Praise for *Origami Dogs*

"*Origami Dogs* folded my mind into a quivering heart. Within its pages, Noley Reid captures contemporary society's terrible turbulence and grace-filled consolations like no one else. To borrow from one of Reid's own gems, these fierce stories are the bubbling, fiery, terrifying, gorgeous 'innards of a volcano.'"

—Ethel Rohan, author of *In the Event of Contact*

"Noley Reid's compassionate collection doesn't shy away from the violent and grotesque, nor the intimate and beautiful. These stories are about pets, yes, but they're also about people—about all of us, really—and how we navigate traumas created by ourselves and inflicted upon others, all while the animals in our lives watch with bewilderment. Always engaging and often harrowing, *Origami Dogs* delivers powerful stories that will stay with you long after you've read them."

—Michael X. Wang, Winner of the 2021 Pen/Robert W. Bingham Prize for Debut Short Story Collection

ORIGAMI DOGS

ORIGAMI DOGS

STORIES

Noley Reid

AUTUMN
HOUSE PRESS

NAMES: Reid, Noley, author.
TITLE: Origami dogs : stories / Noley Reid.
DESCRIPTION: Pittsburgh, PA : Autumn House Press, [2023]
IDENTIFIERS: LCCN 2022045494 (print) | LCCN 2022045495 (ebook) | ISBN
    9781637680643 (paperback) | ISBN 9781637680650 (ebook)
SUBJECTS: LCGFT: Short stories.
CLASSIFICATION: LCC PS3618.E5453 O75 2023 (print) | LCC PS3618.E5453
    (ebook) | DDC 813/.6--dc23/eng/20220928
LC record available at https://lccn.loc.gov/2022045494
LC ebook record available at https://lccn.loc.gov/2022045495

Printed in the United States on acid-free paper that meets the international standards of permanent books intended for purchase by libraries.

Autumn House Press is a nonprofit corporation whose mission is the publication and promotion of poetry and other fine literature. The press gratefully acknowledges support from individual donors, public and private foundations, and government agencies: This book was supported, in part, by the Greater Pittsburgh Arts Council through its Allegheny Arts Revival Grant, the Pennsylvania Council on the Arts, a state agency funded by the Commonwealth of Pennsylvania, and the National Endowment for the Arts. To find out more about how National Endowment for the Arts grants impact individuals and communities, visit www.arts.gov.

For the whisper-snout snufflers
whose hearts have taught me nearly everything I know,
Henrietta, Bugsy, Ruthie, Trumon, and Dodg'em

TABLE OF CONTENTS

Origami Dogs

ris Garr rose at four every day before school to feed and water the dogs in the barn. They weren't hers. They would never be hers. She used to beg—how old had she been then? She didn't remember it, just the feeling of the want so intense it was like a rock in her mouth—and then she had to stop or she thought maybe she would die from the sadness of it. The dogs were her mother's and they were money. Right now, there were thirty-seven but sometimes there were only twenty and sometimes there were over fifty. Her mom, Gloria, drove all over Indiana or out to Kentucky or Ohio or sometimes Michigan with her tried-and-true dams to mate them with the best champion studs she could afford, to keep the breeding going and going and going.

The barn had individual pens for each breeding female—Iris could never call them *bitches*—arranged by breed. First came all of the small dogs: the miniature pinscher, Chihuahuas, Yorkies, Westie, and Maltese. Next were the medium dogs: the spaniels, bassets, whippet, and beagles. And then the large dogs: the English Setter, black Labs, the dalmatian. Her mom used kiddie pools inside the pens as whelping boxes and while the puppies were still small, the pools prevented them from escaping and ensured the mother dogs could nurse them all together. They were easier to clean, too.

This morning, Iris found no new litters. One of the beagles was going to start contractions any day now. Iris didn't like leaving her. She lingered some at her pen, watching the dog. In the night, the beagle had made a nest out of the towels in the whelping pool but wasn't pacing or panting yet. Iris checked on the Westie, only halfway through her pregnancy, then walked down to the large dogs, the heavily pregnant dalmatian whose flank rippled with movement, and the Lab litter. Roly-poly seven-week-old puppies that climbed on one another and their mother nonstop, grunting and snuffling. The pool didn't contain them anymore. Iris reached a hand down into the pen and two or three immediately glommed on to her with their needly teeth hidden inside velveteen muzzles. "You poor thing," she said to the mother dog, extricating her hand and rubbing the red marks.

Iris finished filling the water bowls and bottles and poured puppy kibble in all of the food dishes. She kneeled at one of the basset hound's pens because the dog wouldn't start eating alone. "Good girl," said Iris, stroking her long back. Then Iris scooped poop and wet shavings from the pens and put down more bedding and fresh towels where they were needed. The Yorkies always peed all over their towels instead of the shavings and danced circles around Iris's boots while she worked. "It's all right," she told this pen's dog, "I know you can't help it." Gloria said pregnancy was tough on the bladder and the nerves. Iris reached down to move the Yorkie into her pool, but the dog popped right back out and was underfoot again, so Iris simply worked faster. She brushed the two spaniels' ears and the English setter's speckled ears. Her mom kept all the long-coated dogs clipped short but the long ear fur still matted if given the time. The setter licked Iris's knee, the denim covering it, as she brushed. Now Iris shelved the brush and went down the length of the barn, giving each of the other dogs and puppies a stroke on the head, behind the ear, or on the rump, depending on what was accessible, then she went back to the little aluminum-sided house nestled in southern Indiana's rolling hills.

Inside, she sat at the kitchen table with toast and orange juice. She wrote her mother a note:

The beagle's about ready.
Please check on her today
before you leave for work.

By 6:30, Iris was on her bus to the high school. She smiled at the driver, who once whispered to her that a dryer sheet was sticking out of her pant leg. She sat in her regular middle seat. The popular and older kids sat in the back. They talked of love lives—real or imagined, Iris didn't know. They talked of video games and TV shows Iris had never played or seen and knew she never would, homework and tests happening that morning, how Mr. Flynn was a dick to assign three chapters last night. They laughed and said things that made Iris smile and want to be part of them, and even for a moment she shut her eyes and imagined she was a junior or a senior and was with them.

"What stinks?" said one of the girls.

Iris opened her eyes.

Iris heard the tussling of bodies tumbling into one another and more laughing.

She looked down at her shoes, which was dumb since she'd worn her boots in the barn. She touched two fingers to the damp spot on her knee. She didn't think she smelled of dog but she wasn't sure. Carefully, she tucked her nose into her sweater and sniffed. Maybe she should have showered. Or changed her clothes after mucking out their pens. She couldn't tell.

"What did you step in, Grady?" said a boy.

"Me! No way. Check all y'all's feet." Just an hour and a half across the Ohio River, but she could always tell who was originally from Kentucky.

At lunch, Iris sat by herself at a table of other kids sitting by themselves. She ate her burger then smoothed the foil wrapper and folded it into an origami Scottie dog.

"That's cool," said the boy diagonally across from her. His name was Denny McCauley. He was in her biology class, sat way at the back. He had short black hair and every day wore black shirts with a black zip-up hoodie, black jeans, and black Converse shoes. Today was no exception.

Iris smiled. She pushed it across the table to him.

"Thanks," he said.

Iris took her tray and dumped it.

Fifth period was biology and Denny's arm brushed hers when he walked past her to his lab table.

On the bus home, Iris thought of the beagle, hoping she hadn't gone into labor yet. Once there, however, she found the dog shivering through contractions. Iris sat in the pine shavings of the pen, with the dog in its whelping-pool nest. She stroked the dog's back. "That's it," said Iris. "That's a good girl."

The dogs didn't have names. Gloria insisted. She referred to them by the number she gave them when she first acquired them but Iris couldn't bear to think of the dogs as numbers. So they were all just *good girls*.

Now the barn was quiet around Iris and the beagle. It was always like this. Any time a dog whelped, the rest of the dogs and puppies hushed. The beagle pushed and Iris took her hand away but said, "You're doing such a good job." After a while, there was a puppy. The beagle looked back at it then picked it up so gingerly and set it down before herself so gingerly and licked the membrane from the puppy so it could breathe and chewed the cord and placed the puppy at her side so it could nurse when it was ready. The beagle panted and shivered and began pushing again and thirty minutes later, she delivered the next pup. She carried on like this well into the evening's first darkness.

"Iris?" It was her mom coming out of the house, back from her shift at the library, and flipping on the barn's lights.

Iris blinked away the brightness. "Back here," she called. "There are eight already."

"Good job, 27!" Iris's mom clapped her hands together silently and leaned on the gate of the pen. "How many more do you think there'll be?"

"She might be done." All but one of the pups was nursing. It squealed softly like a guinea pig, like the newborns always did. Iris picked up the straggler—all spots and big, round snout—and placed it at a nipple. It snuffled on.

"Have any homework?"

Iris nodded.

"Head inside. I heated you up a dinner to have while you work. I'll stay with her." She opened the gate and stepped in.

"Make sure this one gets milk," Iris said, pointing.

"I will."

"This one. With the white notched spot on the neck," said Iris.

Gloria was touching each pup on the head, counting.

"I said there are eight. Just watch this one. It needs to nurse." Iris stood up.

Gloria stopped and looked up at her daughter. She ran her tongue over her teeth. "I know what I'm doing," she said.

Inside, Iris ate her tray of chicken tenders, mashed potatoes, and green beans while studying genetics and heredity in her biology text. She ran through a table of Mendel's inherited traits, drew out Punnett squares for brown eyes, free ear lobes, non-cleft chin, mid-digital hair, and left-on-top hand clasping, then wrote down her phenotypes and genotypes accordingly. It was the kind of stuff her mom did when breeding the dogs.

She was asleep when her mom finally came in.

"She finished with nine," said Gloria, standing in the doorway of Iris's room and rubbing her neck.

"Are you sure she's through?" Iris sat up in bed. "I can go back out."

"No, you sleep. She's all done. I waited long enough to be sure."

Iris lay down again but couldn't fall back to sleep. Once, they lost a Jack Russell who labored too long. They'd thought she was done, too, and maybe she was. Gloria said she'd waited with her long enough to know the whelping was complete but the next morning when they checked on her, she was dead and so much blood had come out of her back end. They didn't know what happened, but Gloria cleaned it up and put the dog's four lifeless puppies in with a Maltese who'd just had two in a litter a few days earlier. The four were already gone, though, no matter how much the Maltese nervously licked their wet coats to get them breathing.

Now Iris listened to her mother brushing her teeth, running a shower, flushing the toilet, and climbing into bed. And then Iris put on her boots and coat and went to the barn. She sat in her nightgown with the beagle and her sleeping puppies, just to be sure.

When birds began to warble, Iris shook blood back through her limbs and rushed through her chores. At school, when she opened her locker, something fell out into her hands. It was an orange origami cat. Iris smiled. She placed it on the top shelf of her locker while she exchanged books from her backpack. Then she took the cat and slipped it into her pocket.

At lunch, she sat at the alone table and looked for Denny again, but he wasn't there. She ate her burger and folded another dog, this one a Lab with its head up to the sky. She didn't know where Denny's locker was.

"Is that for me?" he said, plunking down his lunch tray.

She looked up. "Oh. Yes, I guess so."

"Does it play well with the cat?"

Iris took the cat out of her pocket and set it on the table next to the dog. "How'd you learn it so fast?"

"YouTube."

"Stupid question," she said.

"McCauley! You playing with paper dolls now?" It was one of the juniors from Iris's bus. Kyle Seaton, wearing a royal blue Gap rugby shirt. "Pussy!" he sneered, and he swiped Denny hard across the back of his head and walked on by.

Denny grabbed his head, his neck. He leaned forward over his untouched food.

"Asshole," said Iris, clenching her toes inside her shoes.

Denny didn't say anything. He pushed his tray away, got up, dumped it all in the trash, and left. Iris picked up the dog and cat and put both in her backpack. In fifth period, he didn't brush her arm when he walked in and his eyes were on his feet.

She was already on the bus when Kyle came on. He'd never noticed her before but today he stopped at her seat. "You're that girl, aren't you?"

Iris felt her pulse in her fingertips, said, "No."

"Of course you are." He ran a hand through his long blond bangs. "What do you mean 'no'?"

What would work here? She didn't know. And all she felt was danger. Her toes rolled under again but Iris looked up at him squarely. "Okay."

He laughed and walked to the back. She listened for her name and Denny's name but it was all *Call of Duty* this or that and Kyle said, "I can't even talk to you right now if you're not playing *Black Ops 4*."

"*Modern Warfare* is killer with the plot twists, man."

"Boys and their guns," said a girl.

"*Modern Warfare* is trash," said Kyle.

At home, Iris sat down in the beagle's pen next to the whelping pool. The dog beat her tail twice. Her pups, bellies full of colostrum, wormed around squealing, trying to hold up their big heads, nursing, and then falling asleep. Eventually, Iris walked all of the pens, feeling all the pregnant bellies for movement, telling every dog and puppy they were good, topping off waters, lingering with the basset so she would finally start eating her neglected breakfast, lifting the Yorkies out of their pee towels, and scooping out poop. She slid a lubed thermometer in under the dalmatian's tail and held it in place until it beeped: 101.3°F. "Not ready yet, girly," she said, stroking the dog between the shoulders.

The next morning Gloria took the whippet to Grand Rapids to breed it and, depending on how experienced the stud was, she might be gone a couple of days. On the bus, Kyle winked at Iris when she walked to her seat. She sat down quickly and lowered herself below the top of the seatback. Then he was there in the seat across the aisle. And then he was there in the seat, next to her, pushing her into the cold dimply wall of the bus. Still, Iris looked straight ahead at the brown seatback in front of her.

Kyle stared straight ahead, too, but she could feel him smiling. "What are we looking at?" he whispered, nudging her softly with his elbow.

"A whole lot of nothing," she whispered.

"Then why are we doing it?"

"Nobody knows."

He nudged her again with his elbow. Again and another time until she cracked a smile and they both laughed. "There," he said, "I knew you weren't a complete robot. Just maybe a cyborg."

Iris rolled her eyes.

"So you're the girl with all those dogs, right?"

She nodded slowly. What was he going to say now? He wanted a free puppy or thought she ran a puppy mill or some other ulterior or nasty motive for sitting here talking to her?

"That's cool."

That was all. Just "that's cool." Iris exhaled. Kyle got up and went to the back of the bus where his friends razzed him about sitting with a ninth-grade girl. The bus heaved itself up the hollow hills of the old gypsum mine. The closer it came to school, the older the houses got. Not historical, just beat-up with cars on blocks in the front yards and broken windows replaced with cardboard and duct tape. Ordinarily they made Iris glum but today, a red dog stood by a moss-stained birdbath and shook in the cold morning sun. She blew the dog a kiss and pressed her hand to the frigid window as the bus passed on by.

At lunch, Iris didn't see Kyle but Denny was there. "Hey," he said.

"Hi," said Iris, setting down her burger tray.

Denny wouldn't look at her. Just kept to the pizza slice and burger on his tray and the windows at the end of the room. She didn't know what to say to him. Especially now, after this morning. She was a terrible person, she knew it. She couldn't look at him without flushing hot, convinced there was some kind of way he knew she'd sat with Kyle, been nice to Kyle, thought soft-hearted things about Kyle. She just couldn't. Denny finished his food and poured his milk down his throat, all of it in one go. Then he set about folding the foil burger wrapper into something. He pushed it to her and got up and left. It was a panda.

"Thank you," said Iris, calling after him, but he was already at the trash.

In biology, she stood out in the aisle, fussing with her books and backpack as students came streaming in. But Denny walked past well clear of her, so she took her seat. She set the origami panda on the edge of her lab table in the hope he would see it there during class or at least on his way out of class and maybe he did but he rushed quickly past her with everyone else. Iris felt so deeply ashamed that she pinched the skin on the top of her hand.

After her last class, which was French, she went to her locker and out dropped a blue origami fox. She turned around to see if he might be near and watching but he wasn't. She held on to the fox, got the right books, shut her locker, and made her way to her bus.

Iris told herself not to look for Kyle. She told herself he was mean. But electric current needled its way through her veins like it had this morning. He wasn't on the bus when she climbed on so all she could do was wish he'd come right now to her. Then reason stepped in, or tried to: She made herself promise she wasn't going to smile when he'd walk by her, though she knew it wasn't a promise she could keep. But then the bus driver shut the doors and started up the engine and Kyle wasn't even on the bus.

At home, Iris did her dog chores and sat with the squealing beagle puppies. She picked up one of them. Its front paws grasped at the air. She stroked its chunk of a head and kissed its sealed eyes. She set it back down and the mother licked it. Iris petted her, said, "You're such a good mom."

The small dogs started yipping and yapping so the medium and large dogs barked and bayed, too.

"Hush now," said Iris. She looked up.

"Hi there." It was Kyle Seaton walking past the small dog pens to come to her.

She stood up and brushed off the pine shavings from her jeans. Now he would know the smell had been her on the bus. "What are—"

"Thought I'd come check out the place," he said and reached a hand in to touch one of the puppies. "Those are like, just born, aren't they?"

"Just two days."

"They can't even see yet."

"They won't for a week or so." She let herself out of the pen.

Kyle started walking down the rest of the barn, so Iris did, too. "Look at those; they're so fat and frisky." He let himself into the Lab pen and Iris followed. The whining puppies, all in their different colored Tyvek collars, were already sold, just waiting to be fully weaned. They clambered around Kyle and Iris, chewing on his shoelaces and the rubber of her boots. They gnawed on fingers that came near their mouths and climbed over Kyle's and Iris's laps when they sat. "How are you not in here 24/7?"

"I don't know, it's work," she said, rescuing the frayed edge of her T-shirt from the yellow-collared puppy's mouth. "But yeah, they're pretty great."

The mother dog laid her head across Kyle's hips. "What's her name?" he said, rubbing her behind the ears.

Iris sucked both lips inside her mouth.

"What's wrong?" he said, placing a hand on Iris's thigh.

She shook her head. She could hardly think now.

"What?" He took his hand back and ran it through his bangs.

"I don't want to say."

"Her name can't be that bad," he said. "We once had a cat called Farty because my little brother couldn't say 'Purple.'"

She laughed. "Those aren't even remotely similar." She longed for Kyle's hand again, even leaned back a bit so maybe he would reach for her.

"I know. There was some evolution of the name over time. Still, it was a bad name."

"Purple wasn't all that great either," said Iris.

"Well let's hear yours, if you're one to judge."

Iris let out a deep breath. "My mom doesn't let us name them. She gives them numbers. She," Iris patted the mother dog, "is 14 because we've had her a long time."

He looked at the dog's face. "14? I guess it's kind of like a name."

"It makes my skin crawl."

He lifted the dog's head off his lap and relocated the

puppies, though they whimpered, back into the whelping pool long enough to stand up and open the gate. "Come on," he said.

They walked out of the barn and went behind it, where there was grass and sky and a stand of redbud trees, purple plum, and cherry trees all just waiting in bud to burst into spring color in the next weeks. Iris felt the top of Kyle's hand brush hers and then he took her hand and held it and they walked to a spot in the grass where the barn blocked the house, on a little hill in the warm sun and cold air near the trees.

Kyle took off Iris's coat and laid it down. He sat and so she did, too, using the coat for a blanket beneath them. He pulled her down and kissed her, moving his tongue in her mouth so she moved hers next to his. When his hand felt along her waist and started tugging up her T-shirt, she let him. And when his hand moved over her left breast in her bra, she let him do that. Then he reached around her and unhooked her bra and she let him do that. Each step seemed so inconsequential, something so small to object to. Managing the list of things to do—keep her tongue moving, moan, eyes shut, hands roving up and down his shoulders like in a perfume ad, hips rocking when he pushed—was like performing the order of operations on an algebraic equation. It felt good, she guessed, but the actual sensation was somehow just out of her grasp. And she was cold, so cold. Then his hand unbuttoned and unzipped her jeans, and she thought, *This is it*, and still she let him do it. And when her underwear and boots and jeans came off and his underwear and jeans came down, and he rolled on top of her, soft and then firm and then pushing in, she let him do it all, and it was one more thing in the equation to perform. And when it was done and he moaned into her hair and fell flat and rolled off of her and she felt the wetness spilling out of her and thought she had done something wrong, she put her bra on and pulled her underwear on and her jeans and boots and coat and said, "I have so much homework," and she ran down the hill and into her house where she turned off all the lights and hid behind the sofa until she was sure he was gone.

Iris fell asleep curled behind the sofa and didn't wake until it was dark out. Then she slipped back into her coat and boots and returned to the barn. She did her night's chores and lingered with the Lab puppies. She stroked the mother dog's head and then, without thinking it through, said, "I'll name you Cleo." She came to the beagle's pen and weighed the pups to ensure they were all gaining, and they were. "Good girl," she told the mother dog, "and I will name you Prudence. There's just something in your wrinkly face."

She stayed in the barn—tidying food sacks, clean bowls, thermometers, all the different sizes and colors of puppy collars, worming medicine, and high-calorie supplement and puppy formula for when nursing doesn't go quite right—to avoid going inside but a little after eleven, Iris worked off her boots and slipped out of her coat. She made herself a bagel and ate it standing at the kitchen counter, though her mom had left a couple of TV dinners in the freezer.

Gloria didn't return that night. She texted: "This stud can't find 32's vulva to save his life! Trying to guide him. Don't know how long I'll have to be here. Everything okay there?"

For the first time ever, Iris didn't answer her mother. She went to her room and stood in front of the mirror on the back of her door. She wiped sleep from her eyes and moved her hair from in front of her shoulders to behind. She couldn't understand it, why he'd come today. Why he'd shown up here and then taken her around back and done what he'd done. With her. She'd never even been kissed before.

She took off her shirt. She undid her jeans and let them fall to her ankles. At least she'd worn a somewhat nice bra, electric blue with a little lace. But the underwear was mortifying: white cotton hipster with little yellow flowers all over. She reached around back, unhooked her bra, and pulled it off. She stuck her thumbs in the waistband of her undies and pushed them down to the floor then stood back up and tried to examine herself through Kyle's eyes. Her tiny breasts and unruly pubic hair. Her plain brown hair and eyes. She couldn't see what would make him want her but somehow, someway, she figured, he did. She wrapped her arms around herself imagining they were his and went to bed naked like this so she could feel him touching her.

In the morning, Iris saw that the dalmatian was nesting. She gave her extra towels in her whelping pool and took her temperature again. "You're cooling down: 99.4. If you can wait 'til 3:30, I'll be right here with you," said Iris. The dog licked her lips and laid her head down between her front legs. "You, I'll name Polly."

Iris finished her chores. She showered and dressed, opting for a pair of silky black undies and a silky black bra. She tried to curl her hair but managed just one curl before burning her cheek. She gave up. She skipped toast and juice and ran to catch the bus. She climbed up the steps and the driver said, "Morning."

Iris said, "Good morning," and started up the aisle, beaming. She looked toward the back of the bus and there was Kyle. Iris practically glowed. She hovered between the middle seats slowly, thinking maybe she would go to the back. Maybe he would come to her again or call her back there. Then Kyle turned to his friends, talking, laughing.

Iris looked away. She took her seat. She let her eyes cross staring out at the hills.

At lunch, Denny asked, "What happened to your cheek?" He touched his own in the same spot and she remembered the burn.

"It's nothing," said Iris, feeling dumb. She put her fingers in the one curl, trying to pull it straight.

He finished his burger and was folding the wrapper when Iris saw Kyle. He was coming to talk to her, to see her. Maybe to sit with her. It had been a misunderstanding this morning.

"Pussy, McCauley!" Kyle sneered and whacked the back of Denny's head. He didn't even look at Iris and he walked on by.

Denny wadded the foil.

Iris teared up but Denny was gone to the trash already and no one else looked at her.

At home, Iris went to the barn. She checked on the dalmatian. Nothing yet. She did her chores. Sat with the whiny Lab puppies, sat with the squealy beagle puppies, spent time with each of the thirty-seven dogs then went inside and curled up on her bed and cried.

"Why aren't you with 6?" said Gloria, standing in her doorway.

Iris had fallen asleep and it was dark now. "Sorry," she said. She started to get up then stopped. "Can't you?"

"I just got here." Gloria took a scrunchie out of her hair, letting it down from its makeshift bun. "I've been driving all day."

"I've had school all day. Plus I feed them. I water them and brush them. I scoop their pee and poop and wipe down their whelping pools. I spend time with them so they know they're loved. I name them and play with them and you—"

"You name them?" Gloria's eyebrows knitted together.

"Someone has to."

"You can't name them, Iris. They're not our pets."

"We've had Cleo for six years. And Polly we've had since I was seven. They're our family, Mom."

"Who are Cleo and Polly?" Gloria blinked several times.

"Never mind. Just you come in after I've done everything for days and next to everything for years, and you want me to stay up all night and watch the birth. And ordinarily, I'd do it—I always do. But not tonight. Just you, I don't know, what do you even do?"

Gloria left the room and Iris stayed sitting on the edge of her bed, running through everything she'd said and hadn't said, hearing Kyle call Denny *pussy*, and the names Cleo, Prudence, and Polly. Seeing her mom let down her hair or rub the side of her neck like she did every time she came home from the library.

Iris pushed and picked at her cuticles. She let out a big sigh and got up and went to her mom's room. Gloria was brushing her hair. Iris hugged her from behind. "I'm sorry," she said.

"You should be." Gloria held the brush at her side. She looked at Iris in the mirror. She was waiting for her daughter to say something more maybe, but Iris didn't know what. Gloria took a deep breath and let it out. "I wish we had all the money in the world—"

"Mom."

"—then we could just have the dogs we want."

"I know, okay?" said Iris.

Gloria turned around and looked at her. "It's a lot of work. I get it, I do."

"It's okay. I'll go."

"You sure?" said Gloria.

"I'm sure," said Iris, turning to go. She stayed in the barn all night with the dalmatian she'd named Polly, watching her whelp seven pups. But there was something wrong. Three of them weren't breathing right. Their bodies were strange, their rib cages too flat. Polly licked clean their membranes and set them in place to nurse and they did but when the other pups fell asleep, these three struggled on for air. They didn't squeal, and maybe they couldn't. Iris went for her mom and when she came and held each one in her hands and felt the flatness of the ribs for herself, Iris knew that they would die and there was nothing she or Gloria or the vet could do.

"Go on to bed," said Gloria. "You'll still get some sleep before school."

In the morning, Iris found her mother with the dalmatian but there were only four pups left. "Why did it happen?" said Iris. They'd only had birth defects three times before in twelve years of breeding.

"It's just a fluke," said Gloria, standing up and letting herself out of the pen. She brushed off the seat of her pants. "Don't think about it."

"Where are they?" asked Iris.

"Don't think about them."

"I can't help it."

"It's just a fluke," said Gloria.

"How can three of them be a fluke? Polly's had probably twenty litters with no problems."

"Do your chores then get ready for school," said Gloria, walking out. "I'm going to bed."

Iris went to Polly. She looked into her dark amber eyes. "I'm so sorry they were sick and died. But at least you have four healthy ones." Polly licked her remaining puppies incessantly as they slept.

On the bus that morning, Kyle ignored Iris again. When she opened her locker, an origami owl fell out and she did not pick it up. At lunch, she was shaky from lack of sleep and food. She ate her burger and wadded up her wrapper.

Denny said, "Don't do that," and then he folded his own into a unicorn and set it on her tray, where she was staring.

She looked up. "I feel like I'm disappearing," she said.

He didn't answer her. He swallowed like maybe he was about to but he didn't say a word. So Iris stood up and took her tray to dump it, unicorn and all.

For weeks, Iris stumbled through her life, pinching the skin on the top of her hand until it went numb. And then the dalmatian puppies turned out to all be deaf and that had never happened before. Two of the beagle puppies had a connective tissue disorder called MLS and three developed with narrow heads and tiny eyeballs.

Sitting at the kitchen counter one night over supper, Iris said, "Who are these champions you're breeding our dogs with? Their people must be scamming you. You should sue them."

"Maybe so." Gloria pushed at the white rice on her plate.

"They're ruining your business. Of course you should sue."

"There are no guarantees in breeding. Sometimes you hit a rough patch."

Iris shut her trig textbook. "Mom, you don't have perfectly good dogs for twelve years and then have three dogs die and nine dogs so messed up we'll have to give them away—if we even can." Iris dipped her last fish stick in mustard and ate it.

Gloria picked up her plate and took it to the sink. She scraped it clean and ran the disposal.

"Mom!" said Iris. "Listen to me. I'm serious. Do something!

Those people ripped you off. Are they the same sires you always use?"

"No." Gloria scrubbed her dish.

"Who was it? Where did you find him?"

"There's a whole formula. You wouldn't understand."

"Are you kidding me? Of course I would understand." Iris took her dish to her mother. "What aren't you telling me?"

"Nothing."

"Mom," said Iris, holding Gloria's elbow. "Tell me."

"Money is tight. The library cut back my hours."

Iris's stomach dropped. She let go of her mother. She felt almost everything inside herself let go. "You didn't," said Iris.

Gloria shut her eyes and stopped washing the rice pot.

"You wouldn't do that," said Iris. "Please tell me you wouldn't do that. That you didn't get some random pet shop dog to mate with Polly and Prudence and whoever else out there?"

"Not random. I wouldn't do that," said Gloria, eyes open again. She dribbled more dish soap into the sink and set about scrubbing intensely.

"Then what?"

"From their lines."

"How close: great-grandson, grandson, nephew?"

"Son," Gloria said softly.

Iris slapped her palm on the counter. "That's not linebreeding. That's *in*breeding!" She shook her mother by the arm but Gloria would not turn around. "What's wrong with you? Of course all the puppies are messed up now. Of course they are. It serves you right. I can't believe you would do that to our dogs, our beautiful, sweet, loving dogs who do nothing but churn out babies for you year after year." Iris threw her plate into the sink. "You horrible, selfish bitch. We're . . . we're a fucking puppy mill!"

Iris slammed her feet into her boots, grabbed her coat, and ran to the barn. She was crying and the dogs were quiet. She walked along the pens, letting each dog lick her fingers. "I'm so sorry," she said. "You don't deserve this." She went down the line of pens naming each and every dog, including the deformed puppies: Lyla, Piggy, Cora, Winnie, Hortense, Summer, Dinah, Millie, Prudence, Bird, Ferris, Franny, Sasha, Wilson, Watson, Dilly, Wayne, Suarez, Sadie, Cola, Camille, Ivy, Edith, Jellyroll, Finch, Myrtle, Thistle, Birch, Aspen, Plum, Muffin, Rose, Soufflé, Margaret, Kristen, Daisy, Alice, Cleo, Isaiah, Marv, Pudding, Missy, Harvey, Essie, Rain, Betty, Sarah, Katie, Eliza, Avery, Bridget, Holly, Delia, Polly, Monroe, Jed, Dora, Valerie, Domino, Burnham, and Celia. And for Polly's three that died: Claire, Ellen, and Clyde.

She got some of the clean towels from the cupboard shelves and made a bed for herself in the pine shavings next to the Westie, who would be the next to whelp. She hadn't nested yet but by the calendar Gloria kept, she was close. What sort of monsters she would have, Iris could only imagine.

That night she dreamed every one of the dogs, that she opened their pens and led them out into the trees. Some disappeared in the distant woods. Others—the recent mothers—kept their puppies with them on the hill. And no matter their defects, all the puppies were there and they all tussled on the hillside, rolling down and climbing back up. For a while, Iris let them play like this but then, in the dream, she could see her mother's car coming up the driveway. She turned back to all the dogs, clapped for their attention, said, "You have to go now. This is your very last chance!" And though she loved these dogs more than any person in the world right now, she waved her arms and shooed them off into the woods.

When she woke in the morning, she was afraid she really had emptied the pens. If she were brave enough or cruel enough, she would have. But no, there was Millie, the Westie, right next to her, pushing through a contraction. "That's a good girl. You can do it," said Iris. She quickly finished feeding, watering, and cleaning, and came back to sit with Millie. And just like that, the dog stopped pushing. She'd always been like that; she preferred to whelp alone. Iris busied herself folding towels with her back to Millie. Periodically, she looked over her shoulder but the dog hadn't even resumed panting.

By 6:10, there was still no pup. Iris ran to wash up, change clothes and shoes, get her backpack, and catch the bus.

The bus driver said, "Morning," and she reached in her backpack and handed him an origami St. Bernard. "Very cool," he said.

Iris never even looked at Kyle anymore, though she thought about the fact that she wasn't looking at him every time. She sat close to her window and watched the hilly southern Indiana farmland—cornfields, soybeans, and fresh subdivisions—go by. Close to school, she looked for the red dog again, but he wasn't out. At lunch, Denny no longer sat at her table. She didn't know where he went, he just wasn't there anymore. Today, after she ate her burger, she folded the foil wrapper into an origami poodle with a fancy lion haircut, and when biology let out, she followed Denny to his locker.

"I made this for you," said Iris, placing the poodle in his hand.

He turned it over, studying it. "Complicated."

"Thanks."

He reached into his locker and came out with all the dogs she'd ever made for him.

"You kept them."

He smiled. "Sure."

"I have yours, too." She dug in the outer pocket of her backpack and came back with a handful of his animals.

"Not the unicorn," said Denny.

"What unicorn?"

"It's fine." Denny put the foil dogs back into his locker.

The bell rang and they both turned and went in opposite directions without another word.

After school, Iris climbed the steps of the bus and the driver smiled big at her. He'd strung a thread through her dog and hung it from his wide rearview mirror. She made her way to her seat. It was bright and warm this afternoon and the St. Bernard danced the sun around the inside of the bus as it spun on its thread. Iris looked away from the reflection, out her window at the next hulking bus parked and waiting to leave the school lot, too. And that's when she saw them. Set up in one of the other bus's windows across and a few seats up from hers, was a line of her origami dogs in a parade: the poodle, Scottie, basenji, collie, pit bull, Boston terrier, all nose to tail. Iris laughed. She picked up her backpack and moved to the seat opposite the dogs and pulled out all of Denny's origamis and stood them in the upper window frame, too. First the panda, then the fox, the gorilla, the bat, buffalo, stingray, and cat. She waved at him but he didn't see her. She knocked and knocked but Denny still didn't look.

Iris took down the origami menagerie and stuffed the animals into her coat pocket. She slumped low in the seat and waited for her bus to move and she went home. Home to the used and broken dogs, the trying dogs, the dogs she would never feel curled up in her bed or tugging at the end of a leash. She stepped down into her boots and sat with the Westie, who had already whelped three pups Iris was afraid to pick up and examine closely. She stroked Millie's wavy, white fur and coaxed her on but it seemed she was done with just three. Still, Iris stayed with her to be sure. She ached to turn all the dogs loose but knew that would be even crueler than this life for them. Instead she vowed to carry on with all her chores, tending the dogs as much as she could to keep her mother away from them as much as possible.

Iris left Millie's pen. She scooped the origamis out of her pocket and arranged them in parade on the cupboard shelf for the dogs. "Here," said Iris, "a little decoration for the barn. Because this really is your home and you are my family." And then she began to call each dog and pup by name again, believing the very act was a gift and a grace.

Shepherd

We don't belong to the house or anything in it. We don't even belong to each other. There are two black dogs and a calico cat we've never seen, and we are here to keep them alive and happy while the family is gone to Antigua for two weeks in June. The house is big enough and has a pool, but Twyla doesn't have cable at her house so, at first, she is glued to the set, watching *Say Yes to the Dress* marathons while I sip margarita mix slushies poolside in my jeans. We arrived on a Sunday and, after picking up the house key from the neighboring farm, where a girl was outside playing tag with a sheep, and stopping for groceries at a tiny market in the one-block downtown, I don't really see Twyla again until she emerges from the TV room Wednesday evening.

I peek in on her just as she's flicking off the remote and standing up to stretch. "Well, that's embarrassing," she says. "My eyes feel hardboiled."

"Nobody knows what they'll do when let out of TV prison." I squeeze her shoulders, feel the days of being bunched up on the sofa in knots there. It's the first time I've touched her since getting here and my stomach's between my teeth.

Twyla is not my wife. She was my best friend in college. We almost had a thing, then we didn't, then we almost did, then we didn't again. We said we didn't want to ruin our friendship but then we graduated and moved away. I married someone else, she dated a guy for eight years, and we ruined the friendship anyway with other partners and time. I'd be lying to say I never think about what life would be like if I'd married her ten years ago instead.

"That feels wonderful," she says, but rolls her shoulders from my grasp and turns around.

That's when I do it. I take her face in my hands, pull her to me, and open-mouth kiss her.

She backs up. "Keith . . . what? What are you—what was that?"

I don't know how to say it. Everything that's happened in the last two months. All the times I tried to touch Denise after the hospital. How her skin felt softly possible in the milliseconds before she'd spin away from me. Then the end of my marriage. The finality of it. I can't talk about it without it all rushing back at me, through me, pulling me back down to the blackest despair of April. I don't know. All I know is *don't think about it, don't talk about it.*

I walk away. Go to the kitchen, get three beers, and take them out by the pool where I sit in the cool, wet dark after tonight's rain. Try not to think of lying next to her in bed, Denise. All those good nights before, her belly next to me. Those few nights after, her hateful back. Sampson, the greyhound, comes and lies at my side. I can't make out his black fur in the night—there's hardly any light pollution here—but I can hear his slow breathing, and that's a comfort.

The next day, I sleep until noon, come out of my room ready to grab hold of Twyla, but she's out at the pool. I watch her swim laps, a finless porpoise. Like a ridiculous seventh grader, I search her movements for any signs of requited affection, but she's only swimming, of course. Finally, she climbs the ladder and towels off. Her hair is darker brown and curly wet, her royal blue Speedo from her college swim team days. She is fuller-bodied now, with curvy hips and a nice round butt. Her shoulders are softer now, too, not the bulky triangle-shaped upper body all the swimmers had back then. She bends down and shakes out her hair under the towel. Sweetie, the beagle mix, stands with her face up inside the towel with her. Twyla drops it so the towel completely covers Sweetie who walks around under it, dragging it, until she gets close to the edge of the pool. Twyla lunges to stop her. She takes the thing off in time and rubs the dog, talking to her, telling her something kind, no doubt, because the dog's tail starts wagging. Now Twyla wraps the towel around her waist, Sampson stands up on his stilt legs, and they all come up to the house.

I slide open the glass door. "Nice swim?" I say, searching her eyes.

"Did you even bring a suit?" she says, because I'm in jeans

again, always in jeans. She slips on a pair of strappy leather sandals left here by the door.

"How's your time compare these days?"

"What, to college?" she says, rolling down the top of the towel at her waist and I remember that gesture from her swim meets. Feel it in my stomach as a flutter of yearning for us both before any of the now happened. "Oh my god," she says, "no comparison. I haven't even seen a pool in probably two years. And the last time was in a hotel at some terrible conference."

"Oh," I say. "Yeah, with vet school and joining your practice and all—I got the Christmas card updates, I know you're so super busy."

"I am, Keith." She shoves me playfully. "I got away, though, didn't I? You said it was important." She touches my arm now and looks me in the eye. "You said 'life or death.'"

I glance away. "Have you seen the cat?" I turn, going to the kitchen. Twyla follows me.

"No, I haven't seen her," she says. "Keith."

"Did you feed her?" I say.

"No." Twyla looks away then back at me, at the dogs, at the stove, at me. She folds her arms across her chest. "God."

Now I turn away. "I'm starving," I say, opening cupboard doors, one after the other.

"You haven't eaten yet?" she says behind me, her voice softening.

I shake my head, push around the boxes of Uncle Ben's,

macaroni, and Bisquick on the shelves. "I would have made you a plate," I say. I shut the cabinet and turn back around.

She gives me a weak smile, says, "I know you would have."

We stand here a moment in silence, with her fading smile and mine, all nerves, growing wider and wider, perfectly ridiculous.

But I check the fridge, glance back at her slick, wet hair, the blue of the roll of towel around her waist like home. "Maybe pasta?" I say, feeling hope lodge itself in the back of my throat. I gulp at the lump of it. Shut the fridge and lean against it grinning at her. "An omelet?"

She purses her lips to the side, thinking.

"There's not much else in here. We need to hit that shop in town again."

"Grilled cheese," she says.

"Yeah, grilled cheese we could do." I rummage in the crisper while Twyla pours kibble in the invisible cat's bowl, stationed on a back counter so the dogs won't get to it. "There's a sad half tomato left and an even sadder half avocado."

"Let's do that. Grilled cheeses it is," she says and gets out the cutting board and tomato knife.

So she's good again, chipper. All's well.

Sampson comes into the kitchen. He noses his empty dish, then stands next to me where I'm slicing the muenster. I give him a piece of cheese and he stands, snout like a periscope at the counter, waiting for the next. Now Sweetie shows up. She whimpers at me so I give her a piece of cheese, too.

Twyla stops cutting the avocado. She is staring at me. "You know they'll just beg for more now."

"But they're good dogs."

"It's really bad for them," she says.

"If it's so bad, why do *we* eat it?"

"Because we're stupid humans who live a longer life and we rationalize that poor choices won't harm us just this once, over and over and over again." She moves on to the tomato now.

"Well, it's only one piece for each of them. Just once and it brought them joy and now they're done."

She looks hard at me. "Just once? And they're done now?"

I look away.

No matter the subtext, the dogs don't know they're done so Sampson keeps his nose at the counter and Sweetie sits in place, whimpering. Twyla rolls her eyes.

I take her tomato and avocado slices and lay them overtop the cheese on the bread. I salt and pepper them and close the sandwiches, then gently set them in the warm, buttered pan. Denise is allergic to avocado. We couldn't even have them in the house. Twyla gets us plates and washes green grapes for us. She pours out potato chips and dries the grapes and portions those onto the plates, too. I flip the sandwiches and they're nicely buttery-golden on top now.

"They smell yummy, Keith."

Twyla and I are here together in the Blue Ridge Mountains, where the skyline is soft like draped, purple velvet and the air is all pine sap, honeysuckle, cow manure, and nightly rain. It's easier not to think about things up here.

My brother was best man for the guy who owns both this house and a Christmas tree farm down the mountain a bit; it's all irrigated plus has a couple of workers left behind to run it, as I understand. I called Mark the night I was looking at too many Valiums—I didn't tell him that, just said it was over with Denise, said she left me, said there was nothing more to say. And that was true. She'd been so angry at me, so full of rage that whenever she saw me, she looked like she needed to vomit. Then two months later, something changed: She went blank, no longer felt anything at all. And that's when she left. There was no coming back from that. Mark was headed here in a few weeks; he said I should go instead.

He said, "Call up that girl from your wedding."

"Who?"

"How can you say, 'who?' The one who toasted you and cried."

I pictured her there in her black dress and silk turquoise heels, her red lipstick. My mom touching Twyla's arm when Twyla teared up. I couldn't recall, and still can't, what she said in her toast. Something about losing her friend, maybe. Take care of her friend? The only man she's ever loved through and through. I didn't know, I was just making things up then. "Twyla?" I said.

"That's the one. Call her, man. Bring her out to the house. See where it goes."

"I'm married."

"Nah, man. Not anymore."

I emailed her. Said I had some vacation time and a favor to do for my brother to housesit out here and Denise couldn't make it. I told her there was a pool and dogs and lots of time for us to catch up. And when she said she couldn't take the time off, I said *I need you*. I said *please* and *it has to be now* and I guess somewhere along the string of emails, maybe I even said *life and death*.

And so here I am not saying any of the things that need to be said. We sit on the screened-in porch with the ceiling fan blowing and the dogs at our feet, watching blue jays divebomb a chipmunk who's gathering cracked corn that Twyla threw out near a woodpile. The chipmunk is fast and small enough to hide in the cracks and crevices between the logs. The dogs ignore both, which only tells me this war has gone on here for many years.

"How's yours?" I say, meaning the sandwich, and Twyla smiles and nods and keeps on watching the dinner theater outside like it's her new TV. "Man, they're really going after that little one," I say.

"She's got all the corn," says Twyla, popping a chip into her mouth and crunching.

The chipmunk skitters into the woodpile, but we can still see her face poking out. Her cheeks are full of corn.

"Think she's going back for more?" I say.

"I think she is."

"She's going . . . she's going . . . there she goes!" The chipmunk runs straight out from the wood to the corn, where two squawking jays strut and one more swoops down from the sky. She swerves to miss the jays, confounding those standing, and the calculation of the one now landing without her in its clutch. Still running at top speed, she must have scooped up more corn because, coming back to the wood pile, her cheeks are even fuller, bulging now a full inch wide from both sides of her head.

"That was epic," says Twyla, sighing.

"Fierce."

The blue jays eventually settle down, eating up the remaining bits of corn.

"Are you going to say anything about last night?" Twyla says. She waits a full minute looking at the birds, then looks at me and says, "Or more specifically, your wife? Keith, I need you to talk to me. Keith."

I don't answer her. I look at the chipmunk, whose swollen cheeks I can still see where she's peering out. Peripherally, I see Twyla exhale and now look at the birds pecking about. So I watch her and it isn't like college, but it's not like now either. It's like an alternate plane, where she and I live in a house with two dogs in the mountains and eat grilled cheese sandwiches and she swims every morning. She is beautiful. In profile, her nose is a little too pointed, her lips wide and thin, her eyes pale green. I let myself look at her breasts—finally, after all of these years away from her—and they're perfect, still. Bigger than Denise. And wet in her suit, they're one of the last spots to dry and the nipples show through the cloth. I turn hot with shame. I look at the dogs then at the floor and readjust my jeans under the table.

We sit this way, with our crumbs soaking in the pale tomato water rimming our plates. Quietly, with our own thoughts.

The jays begin to squawk and jeer. They flap their wings and hop and fly into the low branches of the nearby maple trees. The chipmunk's face recedes into the woodpile's shadows. A girl appears on the walkway to our porch. Sampson's thin tail beats against the floor. Sweetie sits up and bays. "Hush," I say, "hush," and she eventually listens. Twyla sits up straighter. She moves her long wet hair from shaggy in front of both shoulders to sleek behind her back. I stack our dishes and think to run them into the kitchen, but the girl is at the door already.

"Hi," she says through the screen.

"Hello," says Twyla.

"Hi," I say.

The dogs are both at the door, pressing their noses against the screen, wagging tails and butts like mad.

The girl is chubby, maybe nine, maybe twelve years old. She sets her palm there and lets them smell her, saying, "Good Sampson and Sweetie. Good dogs."

"You're that neighbor," I say, getting up with Twyla.

"I live the next farm over," she says.

Twyla pushes open the screen door, letting the girl in. The dogs go nuts wiggling and sniffing her crotch and ankles.

"Sorry," I say. "Dogs, cut it out."

"It's okay." She has one thick hand on Sampson's head, trying to keep it from between her legs, and one hand low on Sweetie's head.

"Come sit down. We're housesitting for the Weigels. I'm Twyla, what's your name?"

"I know. My mom gave you the key," says the girl.

"That's right," I say. "You were there."

"I'm Piggy," she says.

Twyla and I look at each other.

"No really, that's my name," she says.

"Okay," I say.

"Come sit," says Twyla, pulling out a chair for the girl and adjusting her wrapped towel, which is trying to come undone. I notice several Sweetie hairs at the waist of Twyla's suit and I smile.

We all sit down and the dogs go to the girl.

"Sorry about the dishes, we just had lunch," I say.

"Can we get you anything?" says Twyla, moving the plates and glasses away from the girl's place at the table. "Maybe a lemonade?"

"No, thank you."

Sampson stands to the left of the girl and she rubs behind his pleated ears. To the right, sits Sweetie, where the girl scrubs at the dog's extra neck rolls. Already, black fur collects beneath Sweetie on the tile floor.

"There'll be no living with those dogs once you leave," I say.

"Sorry," says the girl. She takes her hands away.

"You don't have to stop," I say.

"Oh, I know," says the girl. "It's just, I'm here for a reason. I need help."

"Oh, yeah?"

"What kind of help?" says Twyla.

"I've lost my lamb?" Her voice trails up like it's a question, then she's petting the dogs again. "And sometimes I'd bring him over to play with Sampson and Sweetie—" they both wag slowly to hear their names, "—so I thought maybe they could help look for him." She scrunches up her nose.

"I mean, they're not trained to find anyone. They're not bloodhounds," I say.

"They're just regular dogs," says Twyla. She reaches out a sandaled foot to Sweetie and nudges her side gently with it. "I mean, Sweetie's only *part* beagle, as far as looking at her goes."

The girl looks down at Sweetie and takes a deep breath. She doesn't look back up. "Well," she says, "I just really need to find Norton."

My heart. The belly.

"I'll go with you," I say, pushing back my chair.

"You will?" says the girl, looking up now. "Thank you!"

"You will?" says Twyla, eyebrows arched. "Of course you will." She crosses her arms.

"Sure. Let me grab their leashes."

What surrounds this property is cow pasture and horse pasture as far as the eye can see. Occasional houses appear and sometimes they're mansions and sometimes they're trailers with three or four rusted truck bodies out in front. It has briefly rained every evening this week and will probably rain tonight, too, but the afternoons are hot. My phone app says it's eighty-two degrees right now, but the sky is cloudy so it should feel more like mid-seventies. Still, the air is thick with humidity like a sponge so it actually feels a whole lot hotter. I'm wishing I brought beer, or water at least. The grass comes up to my shins most places, so I'm glad I'm in jeans, though they're stuck to my skin. The girl's wearing jeans, too. Some places the grass is wet and my tennis shoes slide across it. The girl, in solid work boots, grabs hold of me then.

She pulls a scrap of baby blanket from her pocket and holds it in front of the dogs' snouts. They sniff it all right. "It's his," she says. "For Norton's scent. Like they do in police shows."

"Sure," I say. "Can't hurt."

But then the dogs go sniffing in opposite directions: Sampson along the gravel road and Sweetie across the ditch and up into pasture. She's got the scent hound in her so we follow her and veer into pasture. I don't know how the owner of this land will feel about the dogs traipsing through, so I try to keep us close to the fence line, while still covering a lot of ground and going where Sweetie leads us. It's a balancing act.

"So, how is it you have a lamb?" I ask the girl.

"We raise them for meat," she says, her breaths coming fast, "but this one wouldn't have lived without me bottle-feeding it through the night and all. My daddy said I could have it 'cause it would never be big enough for anyone to bother eating."

I study her freckled face, her thick hands swinging as we march through the tall grass. "What's it like having a lamb?"

"I don't know," she says. "He's kind of like a little yard dog."

"Huh. Yeah, we saw you running around with him that day we got the key. That was quite a sight."

"He'll play chase or he'll just curl up with me if I want to sit and read or something. And he hates broccoli just like me."

I stop stock still and hold the dogs' leashes tight. Fifty yards to the right of us now, begins a herd of muscular Black Angus cattle. Unsure of how they'll react to us or the dogs and vice versa, I don't want to move or speak, but the girl doesn't notice we've stopped. She trudges on. There seems to be no reaction at all from the cows other than them studying us while they chew.

So I call, "Hey, wait! Hey you, wait up!"

The girl turns around and stops. I jog the dogs to catch up with her and almost wipe out trying to get Sampson back down to a walk. I'm tempted to let him off the leash. I'm dying to watch him truly run, but I'd probably never see him again.

The girl pets Sampson, but looks up at me. "You can call me Piggy, you know. It's all right. Everyone does."

I nod and we walk on. We pass the herd, probably fifty head, and a small pond. We climb a low hill, then go back down the other side of it and see the end of this property and the start of the next. Clouds still circle the sky. Sweetie tarries at a fence-post, then walks us to the next and the next. Finally, she makes her way under the rails. Sampson follows and I help the girl over, then I climb over and we follow Sweetie along a bias swath of the next pasture, which we soon realize belongs to horses.

We reach their manure before we reach them and the dogs want to roll in it so I wrap the excess of their leashes around my fists and keep them close enough to me to prevent shit-roll-ing. There are hills to this land, too, and the girl is panting now. I slow us down as much as the dogs allow. An appaloosa comes running over the hillside and stops right in front of us. She stands still. Believe me, we stand still. The horse flares her nostrils and flicks her tail side to side. The dogs don't move an inch. Then the horse gallops away, all mane and tail in her own wind. Now the dogs' snouts go vertical. They don't want to budge, though, just stand sniffing forever. Finally, we get them moving and I hear the girl's raspy breathing again.

"It doesn't hurt you?" I say.

She turns to me.

"What they call you."

"It's just a name made up of letters," she says. "That's what my mom says."

"You said *everyone* calls you that."

"Minus her."

"What's your real name?" I say. In the distance are three horses standing near a barn.

"Essie."

"Can I call you that instead?"

"No, that's my mom's name."

"Oh."

"My dad said, 'Don't give her your name, Ess. Just call her what she is.' Later, just to me, Mom said, 'Joke's on him: We've always loved pigs because they're smart and kind and loving.' So now, it's my name."

I want to say the perfect thing but don't know what that is. About it being okay to ask for more from life, to set your sights higher. Something useful. I guess I'd be a shitty father. All I say is, "Your mom sounds like a really nice lady."

I'm turned around as to which direction we're walking anymore, but far to our left in the distance, we can see rain falling as a soft, gray curtain. Likely, we'll be in it before supper today. I think of Twyla in the pool, swimming laps in the rain. Wrapping the towel around her waist in the rain. Rolling the top edge down. Her hair wet down her back.

"We've been walking about an hour and a half," I say, "do you know a route back that would take us through more ground to cover, but still get us home before that rain hits?"

"We go this way," she says and turns toward the darker skies, but I don't say anything. She's the local and we have time.

We don't talk for a while, then Piggy says, "Your wife is pretty."

"Thanks," I say. "Oh, you mean . . . no, Twyla's not—"

"Oh."

"We're just . . . I don't know what we are."

"Okay."

"Being an adult is complicated."

We walk a while more in silence. More sweat snakes my temples and trickles down my butt crack. Not once does Piggy give voice to the inevitable: that there's no way in hell we're going to find a lost lamb who's got to be in a bear's stomach right now. Or if, by some greatest miracle ever, the lamb is alive, then there is no way possible that we will find him with all these miles and miles of mountain to cover and just one sight hound and one mixed-up scent hound. But I don't say any of this. I'd rather be out here sweating off my balls than go back to Twyla's questions.

"What grade will you be in?"

"Sixth," she says.

"How old are you?"

"Eleven."

"Uh-huh." I slacken the leashes some, as we're out of horse pasture now. It seems we're in a fallow field; the wildflowers and weeds are harder to wade through. We are all panting. "Do you like school?"

"Being a kid is complicated."

"I hear that," I say and pat her on the back, then feel funny for having touched her, wonder if she feels funny about it, too.

We come to a bit of woods at the edge of the field and Piggy sees it first. Tucked up under the low boughs of a wispy pine, is the bloody carcass of a lamb the size of Sweetie. I hold back the dogs. Its abdomen is completely gone to the ribs, three of its splayed black legs remain, the black face and ears are there with some white neck, its unbobbed white tail bloodied.

Piggy kneels down in the old needles in front of her lamb. She touches the wool where it is clean: the forehead, along the spine, one ankle. She does not cry. The dogs jostle against each other, wanting to get to it. I make them sit and keep them quiet, far back from Piggy and the lamb. At first, I think she will pick it up. Pick him up. But no, she reaches beside and behind her for the forest floor's detritus, which she piles in front of the lamb's belly. She moves his feet, now folding them in, each of the three, like he is only curled up sleeping. She fashions last winter's dropped pine needles into a pillow for his head and tears a holly cluster of leaves and berries to place over the holes in his neck. She sits back and looks at him and I can't help but need her to cry. He's perfect now. You would never know this poor boy wasn't whole, wasn't breathing and whole and loved and taken home in someone's arms to be adored for all the rest of his days.

I try to catch my heart before it races away from me forever.

I think of the blue room, the paper gown I wore, the way it softened where I folded, how it rustled less and less as the night wore on. I think of the weight of six pounds-seven ounces when it doesn't move in your hands. I've held babies before. He . . . he was like a small bag of soil, risen whole wheat dough, an old woman's purse. A dead lamb. We could have made him a bed in the needles, too, we could have pretended. Except for the bubbles beneath his skin. The red splotching where the layers separate after death in amniotic fluid. Except for his eyes. Open too wide and like a doll's, painted blue. I tried to close them before the doctor showed him to Denise, but the doctor shook his head, said that's only on TV.

When she is done, Piggy stands up, brushes off her knees and hands, and begins to walk deeper into the woods. So I follow her, but when I pass the lamb, when I walk right next to him and see him up close, I am struck less by the blood and more by the way he looks like a sleeping baby lost a long way from home.

Now Piggy and I are walking side by side again and I try not to speak, but the words come, just as the rain falls through the trees and we hear it ticking off the leaves around us.

"Our baby died before he was born and they can't just go in and take the baby out, you still have to labor and deliver the baby."

Piggy slips a hand into mine that holds Sampson's leash.

"Denise still had to labor for seven and a half hours. And the whole time, we knew he was dead. We had no illusions. And the baby chimes kept ringing over the loudspeaker in the hospital every time another baby was born—a live baby—and with every contraction, ours was deader and deader."

The rain falls heavy enough now that it hits our faces, our bodies, the dogs who blink and blink through it; the dirt path before us goes slick and muddy. I'm crying now but it could just be the rain. We keep walking.

I don't tell her that Denise begged me to make them take him out. She said delivering him would kill her. She said it over and over: "It will kill me, Keith. You don't understand. It will kill me." And I knew it would and that watching that would kill *me*, but what could I do? I couldn't do anything to a bunch of doctors or surgeons. They have their protocol, they have their best practices. They won't deviate. Then she left me.

Piggy squeezes my hand. She says, "You were supposed to be his shepherd and you never got the chance."

I lose it now, bawl. She takes the leashes from my wrists and I cover my face like maybe I can disappear. I can't feel my body anymore. Not my fingertips, not my cheeks. Nowhere the rain touches me, can I feel. I could fall to the ground here and never move again, let the rain pummel my own skin away, erode it from my bones until I am nothing recognizable, until I am nothing, not human. Not me. Not a heart beating, beating, aching.

But then there is a pressure on me. The weight of Sampson leaning his weight against my leg. And then I feel Piggy. She hugs me from the side, which is strange and uncomfortable and kind. I give myself over to it. I heave deep breaths until I don't have to think about breathing, then I wipe my eyes and force a smile for her, this child.

"Here I am, going all Dr. Phil on you when we just found Norton," I say. "I'm not being very sensitive. I'm so sorry."

She stares at me a beat too long, then says, "I figured we

weren't going to find him alive." She holds out Sweetie's leash to me and I take it. "Look," she says, and just beyond the woods now, I see the house, with Twyla somewhere inside.

"Well done," I say.

"We didn't beat the rain, though."

"That's okay, now Twyla won't know I was crying or how sweaty I got."

"Um," she says, squinching her mouth to one side, but she doesn't finish her assessment.

Piggy gets me to the house's walkway just as the rain slackens. She gives me Sampson's leash and says, "If you need me, you know where I live," and points up the gravel road.

"You're a really good person," I say. "I'm sorry about Norton, but no matter what, you're about the best person I've met in a long, long time."

Piggy looks down, smiling, her pretty chubby cheeks pink and wet.

The porch is empty, the table clear of our dishes. All the lights on this side of the house are off. I slip out of my muddy shoes. Twyla's pool towel is draped on her chair so I grab it and first dry off my face and hair, then clean the dogs' paws and bellies. I let them off their leashes and hear them soon after in the kitchen drinking from their water bowl.

The main room of the house is dark, as is the kitchen. The cat's dish is empty, but no sign of the cat. I look out at the pool, where the light rain pings down onto the water. I watch it a good while. It's the kind of thing that reminds you how empty your heart is, how bleak your world, not that I need any help.

I know it's dangerous, but I go knock on Twyla's door, which opens as I do. Inside, she sits on her bed in the gloom. Next to her is her shut and, I assume, packed suitcase.

"Are you leaving?" I say.

"Let's don't kid ourselves." Her hair is dry now. She is wearing a peasant blouse and ripped jeans. Red lipstick. She is stunning.

I take her hand. "Come here," I say.

She stands with me and I pull her close by a finger hooked in one belt loop.

"Unh," she moans, then shakes her head. "You can't just get all sexy like that. You have to talk to me."

She is not mine.

I let her go. "I don't know how to say it."

"What happened, Keith?" she says. "Where is Denise? Why are you here with *me*? You know I've always loved you—"

"What?"

"You know that," she says. "Don't pretend you didn't know I've loved you since Freshman Comp., day one, 'Letters to Your Senators.'"

My cheeks warm. "Why didn't you ever tell me?"

"I told you in a million little ways all four years—oh my god, you're actually blushing!" She pulls all of her hair over one shoulder and starts braiding it. "Remember Homecoming? I asked you to take me, didn't I? Remember Thanksgiving lasagna with my mother? Why do you think I invited you home with me every year? Why would I sneak out and get in the pullout sofa with you? And at every swim meet, why do you think I immediately looked at your spot in the bleachers when I finished each race? And your porcupine boxers—I still have those and wear them. I still fucking *wear* them."

"We were friends, I thought. I guess I was stupid."

She lets the braid fall apart and folds her arms across her chest. "But I have a life now. There's some rhythm and order to it. Even a little love. What you're asking me . . . what are you even asking me? Throw it away or just set it aside for a few more days? I don't even know."

I take a deep breath. I swallow. I think of Denise and her endless questions I never had the answers to. This one, though, this one I think I know.

"And why are we—" she motions between us, "—suddenly okay?"

I shut my eyes. "All the years you've known me, you can't just trust me?"

"I trust you," says Twyla. "I do. But I need to know what I'd be walking into. Surely you can understand that." Sampson comes in and she strokes his long face over and over again. His eyes become narrow slits and then are gone.

"We found the sheep," I say.

"That's surprising." She sits back down on the bed.

I put my hands in my pockets. "Have you seen the cat?"

Twyla forces out all the air from her lungs. Sampson lies down now at her feet. He sighs, too.

"Are you still married?" she says.

"Yes."

"Do you still want to be married?"

"Divorce wasn't my choice."

She's quiet for a minute, then, "That's a really politic way of answering my question."

"Sorry," I say.

"So you do still want to be married to her." Twyla's lips thin.

"That's not primarily what I want, no."

"Why can't you just be honest with me? Why is there all this deflection and incomplete answering? I don't deserve this. You kissed *me*! You begged *me* to come here! But somehow I'm just a backup plan?" She bites her lower lip and now there's lipstick there on her teeth. I love her—god, I love her.

I take a deep breath. I think of all the ways I can say what needs to be said. I try to remember how I told Piggy, but that seems like years ago and I don't recall any of those words now, only the pain of it. The way it felt like I might crack apart into a billion tiny pieces that could never be put back together into anything resembling a man.

Yet . . . yet here I am.

Once more I take her hand. Help her step over the big dog. Guide her to me. We walk hand in hand and I lead her out through the sliding glass door. The dogs stay inside, sit there at the glass, watching us. And there, at last, is the calico cat come to sit beside them, but I don't tell Twyla, yet. The light rain begins to curl Twyla's hair again and dots her white blouse. I sit cross-legged in my already soaked jeans and T-shirt on the cement beside the pool and pull her down opposite me so our knees touch. I lean forward and pull her shoulders, too, so our foreheads touch.

I take her gorgeous, glorious face in my hands, but I do not kiss her.

"There was a baby," I say, my eyes wet again, or maybe that's only the rain.

Movement & Bones

Our dogs won't stop barking at the little man in the yard who is cataloging our trees, telling Teddy which ones are healthy, which are diseased. All I can think is thank god he arrived in a mask today because this is June 2020, the time of COVID-19 and, although we called him to try to save one of our three Norway spruces—the middle tree that turned bright chartreuse last fall—we don't want to die to do it.

Drab female house finches flip out safflower seeds from a wide, plexiglass box feeder we have suction-cupped onto the living room French doors. They flit away. Our resident thrasher hops beneath a tube feeder in the center of the backyard. Teddy and the little man move around to the side of the house, their voices trailing away enough that the dogs settle. Gordon, our bullish dachshund, remains alert, his eyes on me. Sasha, the hound, is on a hassock pushed up against one door. She drifts off now, her head listing against the window.

Until the men are within sight and sound of the front door. Sasha bolts up and Gordon bounds after her. Louder and more fearsome than the last outburst. Until the man and Teddy disappear again.

I am inside because I have no right hand and no right foot, because of the way the car crumpled when my husband and I were hit by a teenager in the rain in late February. It was mid-morning, and we'd been fighting and weren't speaking. But he asked me to go to brunch so we were making up, reluctantly, wordlessly, I guess. He put his hand on mine and I held it. Then he turned at a different street—a wrong one for the restaurant, I mean—and I said, "Didn't you want to take Morgan?"

"I found an apartment," he said. "I paid first and last plus the pet deposit, so the dogs can go back and forth between us."

I let go of his hand and he replaced it on the wheel, as if it had never belonged to me.

"Franny, I'm sorry. I just can't do this anymore."

My tongue went thick. My teeth wouldn't fit together all of a sudden. I rolled down the window even though it was raining. He looked over and he reached for me in a kind of rough way. I put my arm out the window, my whole shoulder. I felt the pinging wet drops—felt like somehow they could save me from what was happening if I could just crawl inside enough of them—and that's when it happened, the speed of hot metal carving me.

The driver, just a teenager, said that he meant to stop. I don't remember anything else about him until nine days later when he came into my room at the hospital. Teddy wasn't sure the boy should be let in. He stood up, like to shake the boy's hand or to punch him maybe. I didn't know who he was. There were always so many people coming in and out of the room. I didn't even know if there was still poop in the bedside commode and I didn't much care—sometimes new nurses didn't understand that they needed to empty it, that that was part of their job, too, after helping me to it and back to bed.

So the boy walked in and right away Teddy was up. I stopped staring out the window at the sad outdoor patio of the restaurant shut down by coronavirus across from the hospital, and the bank and empty fields and highway turning pink by the end of the day. At first, I thought my eyes had turned him pink, too, from looking too long into the remnant sun. But then I saw it was really his face. He had those red cheeks some teenagers get, so full of acne they look colored in with crayons. I felt tenderness for him, and then my face made a small smile, which was the first since the accident.

"You sure you know what you're doing in here?" said Teddy to the boy and he moved to block him now so I could only see my husband's back—which is by no means in itself broad or intimidating, but in that moment it seemed quite large indeed.

The boy answered Teddy, saying, "Yes, sir."

And so they both walked over to me and I swallowed hard because now I'd figured out who this must be. I wiped my nose with my gauzy right nothing and I looked at Teddy and then the boy and at Teddy and my missing right foot screamed in pain between the big and second toes, where the wheel well ripped my foot off, right above my ankle.

Teddy let the boy have his seat at my bedside and he pushed over the big recliner I had to use for my occupational therapy sessions. It still had toothpaste spit on the armrest from that morning, but he didn't care. I loathed the OT routines. And I loathed my left hand.

"I'm . . ." the boy started, then lost his nerve and looked down. He pulled a folded spiral notebook page from his pocket but held onto it. "I don't know what I can do, but I'll do anything to show you—to make it right, I mean." He looked up at the white blanket covering my legs.

We waited for him to say more or to give me the paper, but he did neither.

"Okay," I finally said.

He broke his trance and looked at me.

"You can yell at him, you know," said Teddy.

The boy grabbed his chair's armrests like to hold on for a hurricane.

"But I know you won't." Teddy shook his head.

"You ready, Franny?" Martha, the good nurse, came in with the god-awful wound care cart. Sometimes she changed my bandages twice a day, sometimes just once, depending on seepage.

Teddy stood, set a hand on the boy's shoulder, and said, "You should go."

"No," I said, "He should see it."

Martha already had all the dry gauze off of my arm. When she reached the inner layer, the petroleum-soaked gauze, she slowed down almost imperceptibly, just enough to be careful around my stitches and the drainage tube. Removing that bandage always hurt and freaked me out, so she knew to go quickly because my asking her to go slowly—as probably every single amputee did—only made the painful ordeal last a million times longer. I bit my lip and held my breath.

"Oh, god," said the kid, gulping.

"If you're gonna lose it, step out to the hall," said Martha, glancing at him while she finished.

"Oh, god," he whispered.

Teddy shoved the boy's head between his knees right as he offered up a juicy moan.

"Good call," said Martha. "I don't think he would have made it to the hall."

She had it off now. The way it felt when the moist padding pulled away and finally came free, was like suddenly my hand had regrown there, all light and airy and possible for about two minutes. A tiny fist thumping with blood and muscle, its fingers not quite separated in a mitten made of pins and needles. And then, just as quickly, it would be gone again.

"How does it look today?" I asked.

"Not too angry. The sutures look good. Tube's doing its job."

"Don't talk about the tube," I told her. She knew I couldn't stand the tube.

"Sorry, lost my head." She smiled at me then finished her appraisal. "Puckering isn't too bad. Looks quite good—see for yourself, Franny," she said, preparing a new bandage to cover my wrist and make-believe hand.

"Maybe tomorrow," I said and kept my eyes on the thin, white blanket.

Martha covered my wrist again and wrapped the protective padding and was done. She peeled back the covers to look at the dressing on the end of my leg. "We'll do that one before my shift ends later tonight," she said and then she wheeled out the wound cart and left.

By now, the kid was breathing all right and was almost upright again.

"You can go now," I said.

He walked out silently, or started to, but came back and put that piece of folded-up spiral paper on the foot of my bed. Then he left.

"That was weird," said Teddy.

"Why not just hand it to me?" I said.

"You're right there."

"I'm right here."

I leaned forward to get it and couldn't reach. "It's like a *Far Side* cartoon: *Must Have This Many Hands & Feet to Read This Note.* So Sorry."

Teddy got the note and I read it. The boy wanted to give me his hand and his foot. I mean literally, he wanted to give them to me so a surgeon would attach his appendages to my limbs and I would go on living like nothing had happened to me and he would be the one who couldn't walk or write or comb his hair or cook a meal or ride a bike or fucking play with the dogs outside.

"What's it say?" said Teddy. "Why are you crying?"

"I'm not."

"You are." He got in the bed with me. "I shouldn't have let him come in here. I'm sorry. What the fuck did he say?" He took the paper. Little bits of the ragged spiral edge of the paper flaked off onto the blanket and were instantly lost there but I tried to find them, to pick them up and I didn't know what— preserve them? scatter them to the floor?

He read it. I cried. He cried.

—————————

When Teddy comes in from the yard, he tells me the middle spruce has needle cast disease and will die in a year or two, and so will the other two in a couple more years. But the viburnum and redbud, too, are doomed. They all need to come out. I am stuck in the house because prosthesis fittings weren't considered "essential" in the March and April shutdown, so appointments are all backed up. All I have is a bulky rental wheelchair from the hospital that doesn't even fit in our hallways so Teddy carries me to it each morning and I sit in the living room all day long until he carries me to bed at night. It doesn't make sense, of course, I could sit in any chair just as easily, and it's not as though I can wheel myself around in this, but the hospital insisted we leave with something in order for me to go home instead of to a rehab facility. I could see the trees as a metaphor for the country—the rotting away under Trump—or see the virus as a metaphor for the same—but who needs metaphors when reality is just as frightening? And how did this become about politics? This is the story of our trees dying, our country dying from COVID-19, my body dying in pieces. And our love, somewhere along the way, that died, then wasn't allowed to.

I hear the clink of Teddy getting a beer from the fridge. "Want something?" he calls.

"I'm all right." I don't drink much. If I do, I'll just need him to carry me to the toilet and back. I have one Vitamin Water each day. Teddy unscrews the cap and leaves the open bottle on a table he's set up next to my wheelchair in the morning. Like this, I can hold my pee until bedtime.

I watch the birds. Now a mourning dove and a male house finch share the window box. Sun glows up his red breast and head. The dove is too tall for the box so she has to duck her head while in it, which makes her neck feathers separate into an Elizabethan ruff. She pecks at seed. The finch picks it up. She lumbers off into the air. He stays a while. Two female finches join him. He jumps at one of them and she flies away, too.

Teddy comes in. "Bird-watching again?"

I nod.

"Want the remotes? Or a book or something?"

"What are you going to do?"

"Nap," he says from the doorway, yawning.

He teaches third grade so he's off for the summer, even though we're quarantined. Not everyone is, of course. Crazy people two houses down from us had a huge party last night, no chairs six feet apart—throngs of people everywhere, standing shoulder to shoulder, food tables packed tightly together, smokers standing at our fence line laughing, music to all hours. Teddy walked the dogs out the front door and went in the opposite direction of their house, but he couldn't avoid all the parked cars and people who belonged to them running out to retrieve a phone charger, leaving early, or arriving late. I made him wear two masks and he crossed the street whenever he saw people coming at him, so he came home and described the walk as a constant zigging and zagging to avoid aerosolized droplets. Then all night long, Gordon and Sasha circled and barked at the French doors 'til Teddy carried me to bed, my naked pink and puckered stumps feeling strangely light in the air, like a sawed woman magic trick who can't be put back right.

I was a ninth-grade English teacher. I don't know what I am now. Teddy's dad is a lawyer and he had us file disability paperwork right after the accident. It was just approved this week so I guess I'm officially disabled. He also had us get a lawyer to sue the driver's insurance company for everything I've lost. Some days I sit here and catalog all that is. Some days, it's a list in dollars. Some days, it's a list in words. And some days, it's a list in movements and bones.

I am a still body now. I sit here all day and I grow. I've

stopped wearing jeans because I have just one hand, but even if I had two, the waist wouldn't close. And one of these days, the jeans I'm not wearing would stop zipping all the way up. The occupational therapist in the hospital tested me on dressing. Teddy had brought a pair of sweatpants and a loose T-shirt for me to go home in. I'm awkward and lurchy, balancing on my left foot, standing to dress, but I could pull up the pants' waistband a little bit at a time: the left side, then the right side, then the left side, then the right side, reaching around with my left hand to get the sweatpants up all the way finally. And the shirt I managed pretty well, even using my bandaged stump to open it up the way one normally does with a shirt.

So I dress like a slob now in loose sweatpants every day so that I don't have to ask my husband to pull up my undies and pants, so I am not even more of a chore to him, so I am not more to resent because how can I not be someone he loathes to hear call his name. And these loose pants are getting snugger by the day. I wear my shirts untucked, of course. Let him think the state of my dress has more to do with my competency than my growing size.

Teddy yawns again. "What do you need?" he says. "Do you need to pee?"

"No," I say, too loudly. *I never need to pee! Haven't you noticed me trying to minimize your burden?* I take a quick, softening breath. "I'm okay. Could I please have my laptop, though?"

"Sure," he says. He fiddles a minute with untangling the cords on the floor, then brings it to me. "Just set it here when you're done." He clears a spot on the table next to me. "You've got your phone, it's charged—" he flips it over to check, "—okay, good, and you're sure you don't need the bathroom?"

I nod.

"Okay." He smiles, but it's the look he gives his third graders: protective, wary, proud, helpful, and disappointed all rolled into one face.

He goes to the bedroom and shuts the door. Within minutes I hear him snoring. Gordon's long body is stretched across a patch of sun on the carpet. Sasha is curled up in a sunny bed against one of the French doors. Momentarily, she opens her eyes then shuts them again and she both wags a couple of times and grinds her teeth twice as she drifts back off. I open my computer, order eight loose-fitting jersey dresses. Then I spend the day researching different types of prosthesis hands: the hook, the dummy, and the bionic.

———————————

Tonight in bed, I lie here with my book propped on the special reading pillow Teddy got me so I don't have to try to hold it one-handed. But I don't read. I let out a deep breath. Sasha is curled up against Teddy's thigh. She re-tucks her nose into her tail. Teddy is doing a crossword.

He was doing one the first time I saw him, in the teachers' lounge when we both taught middle school and I was new to the district. He gave me half his pastrami and swiss sandwich because, in all my excitement, I'd forgotten to pack a lunch. Half of his carrots and chips, too. Then he asked me, "Oh man, who wrote *Lasher*?" He came around the table and sat next to me and showed me the clue: *'Lasher' novelist's favorite food?* "It's 22 across," he said and pointed to the boxes, where he already had: _ N _ _ _ I _ _ P _ L A _.

"That's Anne Rice," I said and he started to write in her name. Then we looked at each other. "Pilaf!" we said. After that, we did the puzzle together at lunch daily and shared whatever we each brought to eat 50/50. He'd come to my classroom to pick me up for lunch and my students oohed and aahed. We were dating at work and dating outside of work, seeing movies, going to dinner, cooking for each other, taking weekend trips to Louisville, Nashville, and St. Louis. And always we'd pick up the *New York Times*, or at least the local paper, and do the day's crossword. We even woke up and did the one on the morning of our wedding. But that was four years ago and I can't remember when we stopped or how or why.

I sigh and now Gordon, stretched out lengthwise and up against my right leg, sighs too.

Teddy looks at me. "You did your exercises, right? Are you having pain again?"

Well, there's always some pain, but no, that's not this. I shake my head.

He goes back to his puzzle.

"Got any clues you want help with?" I ask.

He pencils in two letters. "No, I'm doing all right. Thanks, though."

"Huh."

I watch him move through several more clues without writing anything into their boxes.

"How about now?"

"I'd really just like to do this on my own," he says. "You know what I mean."

"Sure."

He writes something down but lightly, tentatively. Just to show me he's getting somewhere, but he isn't really. I think of the car instead, before the metal.

"Why don't we ever talk about it?" I say.

"It?" he says, still studying clues.

I wait for him to understand. But he doesn't.

"About what you said, in the car?"

He stops writing and looks at me. His face blank.

"Getting an apartment."

Softly he says, "I know what I said."

"We've never talked about it."

He shakes his head. "It's moot now."

"You don't have to stay just because I'm broken."

"Don't say that." He sets a hand on my right upper arm.

I look away. "It's been four months. You never even touch me."

"I touch you." He squeezes my arm.

"There," I say, pulling my arm free, "but never down *here*."

I wave my right wrist. "Or *there.*" I lift my right leg under the covers. Gordon lifts his head, then sets it back down.

"I don't want to hurt you."

"You don't want to *hurt* me. Are you serious? Are you fucking serious!" I close my book, set it on the nightstand and dump the reading pillow onto the floor. I turn off my lamp and move down beneath the sheet. I roll away from Teddy and shut my eyes. Gordon pushes into the recess my bent legs now make.

Trapezium,

Trapezoid,

Capitate,

Harnate.

Scaphoid,

Lunate,

Triquetrum,

Pisiform.

Metacarpals, five.

Phalanges, five; their distals, middles, and proximals, too.

"Franny," says Teddy, "Listen, I'm sorry. I don't know what I'm supposed to do. This is all new to me, too." He moves his body up against mine, as much as the dogs in between our legs allow. He nuzzles my neck. He touches my arm again. My elbow. The middle of my forearm. The last two inches of my arm. My wrist. My stump. He wraps a finger around it, then another and another. Then his hand cups it and he holds it. At first his touch is needly, somewhere in between pain and itching. Then, though he does not squeeze my stump, it almost feels like what's there has a beating heart.

In the morning when I wake, he and the dogs are gone from the bed, as usual, and my own hand is wrapped around my stump. I text Teddy that I'm awake and he and the dogs come to get me.

He sets down his 9 a.m. yardwork beer and carries me to the toilet. "There's aphids everywhere," he says. "On the quince, on the roses; they're even on the weeping crabapple. I've been spraying."

"Sorry I can't help."

"Yeah, that sure does suck," he says then grins. "Don't worry about it."

I wipe and he flushes. With me still sitting on the toilet, he fills the basin we use for me to wash my hand and stump. Warm water feels so strange on it. Sometimes it burns. Sometimes I feel my right hand cramping up. Then he loads my toothbrush for me and I spit when done. He squirts moisturizer into my palm and I rub it into the puckery scars of my missing appendages.

Teddy has to do everything now. Carry me everywhere, get my clothes, hook my bra, unhook my bra, pick up my clothes, laundry, cook, clean (or not), refill the birdfeeders, mow the lawn, feed and walk the dogs, go get curbside pickup groceries, and every last little or big thing I'm not thinking of around here. It isn't fair, of course. Though I'm hardly sitting around eating bonbons, I may as well be. Still, this is where we are and we settle into a sort of routine.

In July, we have the spruce torn out, the viburnum and red-bud, too. All over our backyard there are huge gaping holes left in the landscape, just, of course, as there are on my body. Just, of course, as there is in our marriage. We don't talk about it. And nobody calls to schedule the filling in of my body or the filling in of our trees, though we've settled on a hemlock to replace the spruce, because it's a native species and flora that will thrive in this particular climate's heat and humidity, this particular climate's rage and hostility, this particular climate's grief and regret.

The dogs have taken to sleeping in the trees' holes. They dig them a little deeper, a little wider, a little fresher and cooler, then hop down in and sleep for hours. Sasha sleeps in the spruce's shaded hole. Gordon loves the sun so he picks the redbud's, and we don't see either dog until late afternoon when they're hungry and thirsty and come to the back door now, wide-tongue-pant-ing, covered in dark earth and clay, wagging and proud.

I stifle a laugh, looking at the muddy smudge Gordon's nose makes down low on the glass door. Sasha's looking into the sun, her tail beating steadily where she stands behind him. I set down my pencil and clipboard with the alphabet under tracing paper. "You need to fill the holes," I tell Teddy. "They can't come in here like that."

"Where am I going to get a dump truck full of dirt right now?"

"Then keep washing them every time they go outside and want to come back in."

"This is ridiculous," he says, getting up from his book. "It's bullshit."

"Fuck yeah, it's bullshit. Do something about it."

Teddy storms out to the kitchen and out of the house to go hose off the dogs for about the twentieth time this week. I pick up the clipboard and start tracing letters with my left hand again. It doesn't feel like writing, but like shape-making. Like my brain doesn't register anything my left hand can make as holding the potential for meaning words. I trace a line of shaky lowercase *c*'s, that just look like terrible backward commas, and then toss the whole thing away.

I stretch my legs, extending them both straight out, and can't help but see the obvious. An ankle moves its foot in six different ways: dorsiflexion, plantarflexion, inversion, eversion, medial rotation, and lateral rotation. You never think about any of them unless you wake from a coma and have to relearn walking. I work my right calf muscles to rotate my foot at the end of my ankle, if I still had an ankle, if I still had a foot.

The dogs come in, running through the house to get to me, and they put their moist snouts in my hand and butt their noses against my right wrist. Then they shake out their wet coats.

"Sorry, I forgot a towel." Teddy stands in the doorway.

"I see."

Sasha takes up her spot on the window hassock and Gordon stretches out in the sun on the floor again. "God, that thing will take forever to dry out," I say.

"Sorry," Teddy mutters.

We don't say anything more for a bit, but I think of things I could say. Stupid things. Angry things. And things he could say or should say. But the fact is, where are we going to get a truckful of dirt right now if we can't even get one tree planted? Or a foot and a hand made? Everyone's gone nuts in Arizona and Texas; Black people are being strangled, shot, teargassed, and beaten by cops at protests in cities all over the country; Trump has sent unmarked troops in unmarked vans to round up and detain protesters in Portland; COVID cases are spiking, but our governor here in Indiana won't even mandate masks; and people keep moving, moving, moving about, so no dirt in the yard, no hemlock, and no foot and hand.

"Want to stream something?" Teddy asks.

"Sure," I say. "Move me to the sofa."

We sit together and Teddy even holds my hand while we watch another British police drama and I don't know why, but I turn to him and I kiss his neck and his ear and I sort of suck on his earlobe for a second and then I kiss his lips and we French and we haven't Frenched in probably at least eight months. And then while we're kissing, I reach for his shorts, the waistband, the button, and I manage it one-handed, but the zipper stalls midway on a fold without a second hand, so he helps.

Then that changes everything. I don't want to be doing this, but I'm still doing it. Because I'm an adult and I started it and I can't just run off. And stopping would be embarrassing and probably more excruciating than just finishing up. So I push his boxers down and whiff the faint sour of skin that lives on other skin and isn't freshly showered. I pull out his penis and work it in my hand while we kiss, feel it grow and firm up as his breathing shallows and quickens.

I stop kissing, say, "I can't squeeze the top of your balls at the same time anymore."

"That's okay," he says, shutting his eyes. He cups my cheek and kisses me again, then reaches up my shirt and touches my breast inside my bra.

I lean over and finish him in my mouth. The taste is too much sweat, metal, and watery spoiled milk all at once. I swallow.

Teddy turns the show back on, but I can't concentrate on it. Someone new is dead and someone else is suspected because the last suspect is now dead, too. I've missed too much. I watch the feeder birds. A particular cardinal that visits every now and again. He has no crest and his head is nearly all black featherless skin. We call him Wendell. He eats two seeds and flies out to the tube feeder. A female cardinal is out there, too. Maybe she came with him. I hope so, that he has a partner, someone to love and love him. I glance at Teddy, thinking to point out that Wendell is here, but he's engrossed in the show. The forensic pathologist is performing an autopsy on an old man while talking to two detectives, all of them wearing masks to fend off the smell or protect the evidence from contamination.

At dinner, I ask Teddy if he's afraid for fall.

"Of course I am," he says. He takes another bite of his soft flour taco, from which the contents back out the other end and slump onto the plate. "How do I keep eight- and nine-year-olds from touching one another? How do I stop them from sharing food? From whispering in each other's ears? How do I make them keep their masks on? They can't even remember to wear a winter coat to school on days when it's freezing cold out; how do we count on them to remember to bring their mask every single goddamn day?" He puts down the taco and his eyes shine under the hanging light. "And how do I stop from comforting them when someone at the school—a teacher or a schoolmate—tests positive and winds up in ICU and dies? How do I stop them from hugging one another? And how do I stop myself from hugging the child who comes to me crying?"

"Oh, Love."

His eyes are wet. "I'm not that strong."

"It's too much to ask of teachers."

"It's too much to ask of children."

I touch his hand. "Yes," I say. "It is."

He clears his throat. "I'm just glad you're not going back in a classroom," he says. "You'll be safe. That's good."

"Unless you bring it home."

"Right," he says. He gulps his beer and looks at his plate.

"I'm sorry. I need to think more positively."

"There's something to be said for being realistic." He takes another gulp.

In bed tonight, he leans over to kiss me once then whispers in my ear, "I want us to have a baby."

"What?"

He pulls back and waits for me to believe him. "Come on," he says.

"What?"

"Let's do it."

"There's so much uncertainty," I say slowly.

"Yeah, but . . ."

"We don't have any idea if there will ever be a vaccine."

"I love you," he says.

"And there's that."

"I do, I love you."

"What about before?" I say.

He shakes his head. "I don't know. I was . . . I don't know. I can't explain it."

"You got an apartment, Teddy. You were as good as gone."

"I'm sorry." He sits up now. "But that's done." He looks back at me. "It's done. It was a mistake. It wasn't real. I don't know what it was, but it wasn't real."

"Do you still have the apartment?"

"I broke the lease. I got out of it."

"You don't understand," I say.

"What? Tell me."

"You don't understand: How will I ever know which part of our life is the real one?"

And this is when it happens. When the weight of these months—of his apartment, the car accident, my ruined bones and missing pieces, the months and months of seeing no one but a man I love but cannot trust while the universe implodes outside these walls—when the weight of my world finally comes crashing out of my heart.

I sit up, sobbing. I throw his pillow at him. "Fuck your apartment!" I scream.

"I know," he says, trying to hold the pillow, but I have it again and I swing it at him hard. Again and again, I hit him with the fucking pillow. "That's right, Franny," he says. Tell me to go to hell."

Again and again I hit him with the pillow. Again and again I see his face then I don't see his face. I see his face then I don't see his face. And each time I see it, his eyes are closed and his bangs have blown down across his forehead. I see him, I don't see him.

I hold the pillow and wipe my nose on it. "Fuck your apartment," I whisper. I hug the pillow and cry into it.

Teddy touches my elbow then my stump. "I haven't left, have I?"

"So I'm supposed to be grateful? Poor, hideous me?" I sniffle.

"No, I just mean: I'm here," he says. "I didn't leave. I would have left if I wanted to—accident or no accident, stumps or no stumps."

"Are you sure?" I pull my head up from the pillow, tears

stopping, lips in a snarl. "You'd have to be a colossal asshole to do that, you know."

"Yeah, but by now I would have," he says.

"Even before I get my prostheses?" I say, "I can't even walk or fully dress myself! You're a total dick."

He turns his whole body to me. "Franny, I haven't left you."

"But you would?" My eyes tear again.

"But I haven't!"

"But you would!"

He covers my mouth with his hand. "Stop it," he says softly. "Shh. I love you, Franny. You almost died. I couldn't believe it. That I was going to leave you, leave our love. And you almost died, but you didn't." He presses a fingertip into my chest. "You're here and I'm here with you." He replaces his hand across my closed mouth. "I lost my mind along the way somewhere, but it's back and I'm here. I'm not going anywhere without you."

He takes his hand away now, but I don't talk. I sit here looking at him, my eyes still wet. Finally, I reach for him with my right arm, feel his smooth chest against my stump, his bristly neck and cheek, his wispy, long quarantine hair. And I wonder when was the last time I felt something, truly felt anything? I pull him to me and we kiss softly again and again.

How Trees Sleep

Picture yourself at age six, seven, or eight: braids for pigtails, barrettes with the skinny ribbons woven through and hanging in a notched, plastic bead. Sometimes curlers but your hair won't hold a shape, never will.

Picture your home at this age: the sad grayed siding, the shutters nailed in place, the echoey tin carport.

Picture your mother, your father, your sister, your brother: her hair combs and wedding ring set you spin free of her finger, its knuckle, to pretend someone out there intends things toward you; his chef's apron you picked for the silkscreen of the dog there on that pocket, "*chien*" it says, and you practice this word; sister's books always bedside, always torn and folded to mark where she is when you come in the room and she looks up; brother's Star Wars figures in the dank green tent out back, you permitted to play when he is patient or lonesome.

Picture your dog, your cats, your pet crow and rabbits: these last who freeze despite satin-trimmed blankets 'neath the tarpaulin draped over their cage, the ones you stop looking in on come February's ice because you can't bear to touch death by mistake.

Picture your kitchen: where the stove stands, the fridge; picture someone bending to see catch of a blue flame, her stirring a pot of fudge or his awful stew, maybe icing a cake on the countertop as when you broke your wrist skating with the dog who chased the ducks and the three of them—not your father—made the cake in the shape of your cast, even graffitied it identically with your classmates' names and the dog's apology.

Picture your bedroom, your bed, the view from your window: frost in the treetops and stars winking out. Picture your pillow and how you lie in bed. Picture your thoughts becoming dreams as you finally sleep.

Picture the blackness of your room when you wake in the night. How you move through the hall, stepping over the dog who only shifts his chin as you pass. Picture yourself at the door, your hand turning its knob.

Picture the slope of Daddy's side to you—it's what you see first, coming in, his share of the bed—she, near the wall, just enough path for you to slip in there between bed and window to watch her, flat on her back, the covers tight at her chin and beneath her wrists because she is like that, needs things to be certain. You at their bed, standing, waiting, maybe reaching a finger because you're older now and they think you don't need this. Picture yourself wanting to fill the trough between them, wanting to kick off their covers because the trough is thermal, wanting to drape your arms and chin and dreams over her.

Picture yourself asking. Picture your hand, its size—its impossible smallness—were you ever such a child? You're at her side. Hers. You passed him to find her. Because he's a log, a brick, a heavy, heavy stone. And because somewhere, you think, somewhere in her head's sifting through the day and its worries—you're convinced she does not dream—somewhere in there, she knows what it is to feel echo.

Picture your hand over the covers, over her heart. You bending to smell the sour yeastiness of her scalp, tomorrow morning her hair appointment. Your cheek to hers so warm and suddenly you're reminded of the possibility of heat, wish you'd thought of socks. She does not move, doesn't make even a single push for waking to you there. Picture the night across her lips, her lashes so black with it. Picture her young like this, as you know she must have been. Picture her still. She will wake if you speak. If you ask, you know she will.

Weigh this.

Picture yourself unsure. Yourself doubting. It's what you've always known. Because you aren't little or big, not frightened or brave; you just want more. Time and words, her breath near your face because you're on her lap pretending to read along, but really, you're counting her heartbeats, matching pulses, turning your finger in her hair and letting it tangle in your own. Spinning the batter bowl to scrape all the Bisquick from the sides and into the yellow glop, hoping she'll see you've done it right and won't take the spoon and say she needs to get a feel for it herself. Her behind the newspaper, sitting in your tiny, painted chair in the corner, her knees breaking at such an acute angle; she not answering your questions—*Can we have bacon for breakfast? Does a new moon see itself? If I die in the night, will you be extra sure I'm really dead and not bury me, or even move me, for at least a week, just to be sure?* You are supposed to be falling asleep. Eventually she'll give up and declare sitting in your room until you're out at cross-purposes with you actually sleeping. You know echoes, too.

She sometimes tells you things that make you believe she loves you best of the three: that she nursed only you, fed you any time you peeped; that her water broke in a JCPenney's and she was calm; that you were born with your father in the room (for the first time ever) in a home for unwed mothers, and the nurses were good to her and cooed to you, and your father smiled and held you first; that you make her feel like the innards of a volcano, sometimes.

You can see the import of all this, all of it.

So, you don't say her name, don't say a word to her tight, sleeping face because even so young, you've already a strong sense of pushing your luck with her.

Picture yourself in the hall with its Persian rugs and moping dog not even shifting this time but watching you with one eye.

Picture the night still in your room, your own covers unfamiliar. You lying down, you on your belly with your head to

the left. Lift, press, lift again to keep from feeling the carti-
lage in your ear giving up its form. Feel the slowness of your
blood creeping through you now. Forget to feel your ankles,
your knees.

Picture yourself lying just so, letting sleep come again, thinking of her and how little it would have taken for you to whisper
Mother. Or how much. But you didn't. Know that. Because you're
older now and they think you shouldn't need this anymore,
think there's an age when you'll stop wanting her close, stop
waking in the night feeling its blackness the way the trees must,
absorbing it through your skin, all that emptiness. They think
you'll change and start believing you are full instead of hollow.
They trust you'll stop worrying they'll find you dead but not
really dead and will bury you alive and once again, you'll wake
in the darkness, still unable to breathe. They fool themselves
thinking you aren't yet you. That what you need is only what
you want, like a third piece of garlic bread or the new Madame
Alexander Dutch girl. They think they can teach you to need
less. But soon he'll be gone, so what in the world do they know
of what you need?

Instead, picture yourself at last asleep. Easy with your
thoughts and easy with the night across your own face, turning
black your lashes, allowing some moon on your cheeks. Picture
yourself dreaming, breathing that night.

Once It's Gone

There's a gang, or pack—Jesus, what do you call a slew of wild housecats?—of three-legged feral housecats that terrorize the neighborhood trash cans. Five cats. Each with a different leg lopped off except for the fifth, of course, which is missing its tail. They prowl the driveways on trash night, setting all sorts of commotion going, what with their missing legs making them tippy and the way they rub against the cans to knock them down. The neighborhood's lit afire: the Westies jump out of their sleeping-nests and onto the sofa backs, yapping in their front windows; the Airedale gruffs on his chain; our collie paces the backdoor.

Noreen, a little old lady across the street feeds the cats. Not out of pity; these things are beasts. I'm not sure why, but she lures them onto her drive with dollops of mayonnaise, which apparently, cats like very much. When Meg and I see them, their whiskers glisten from so much fatty oil and licking.

Meg and I are old—nearing fifty—and trying not to get fat(ter) so here we are tonight, it being Thursday, out walking the neighborhood when Noreen calls to us, "Oh lookee, lookee!" She's at the Weber and shaking a spatula and tongs in the air. Truth be told, Noreen is the one person we pray we won't see on these post-supper walks. Maybe what I can't stand are the orange and yellow plastic dahlias in pots that line the pathway to her front door or the porch swing coated and overcoated in rust-bubbled white paint. Or maybe it's just her.

Before I can take hold of Meg's arm to gently keep her in the road, she's off neutral ground and heading up Noreen's driveway just like the cats.

"You two are simply charming, the way you go out walking," hollers Noreen. "When Richard was alive, we liked *The Wheel*. Now I can't even spell right since he's gone."

"You miss him, don't you?" Meg's good at stating the obvious in a way other people find comforting.

"But where is Abby tonight?" says Noreen, not minding a few flare-ups from the fire. "I loved to see her ride her little blue bike around with you."

"That was twelve years ago, Noreen. Abby's nearly seventeen," I say. "She zips around in a car now."

"I'm not a dingbat," she says, "I was just saying how nice it was seeing you all together. What a happy family you were."

Meg shields her eyes against the rim of orange light sinking behind Noreen's roofline, says, "Abby's swimming with a friend tonight."

Maybe. That's what she told us when she asked to stay out

late. This is June. School's done, so she's been staying out late with friends all week, and I'm beginning to wonder if we haven't lost some essential grip as people who matter to her. She leaves the house before we get up in the morning and comes home after we're deep asleep. She phones periodically to check in, get approvals. I miss her. I haven't said that to Meg because she's been saying she couldn't wait until senior year came and then college so we could have the house and our love life back. Me, I'm a little scared Abby will go and never look back.

I'm not Abby's real father—a fact I'm the only one remembering around here. And that's big of them, maybe. But a little disorienting, too—like if you just believe a lie hard enough, it's the gospel truth. Kind of makes you wonder what's wrong with lying if it can be undone so easily.

I suppose I need to explain a bit.

It used to be that Meg hated her mother with such fury I thought I could feel the prick of fangs when she kissed my neck. Meg didn't want kids and that was the only thing her mother ever talked about, so I wore a condom each and every time. By association and probably because it was easier to believe I was the bad guy instead of her own daughter, her mother hated me. For ten years it was like that. Then Meg got pregnant and I thought I'd leave. I thought so, planned so, had moved out long before she was showing, but there was some chance it was mine, right? A hole in the rubber? Splash-back upon removal? So when Meg phoned panting, I hesitated then went to the hospital. And when I held Abby, Abigail, when I smelled Meg's blood in this baby's hair, I came back, completely.

You don't believe that, right? Too easy? Or too hard? Maybe if I'd been nineteen, twenty-six even. But thirty-one was different. I'd been with Meg ten years and realized I could walk away with nothing, nothing to show for that third of a life. Still, she'd broken me. Another man inside her—all that shit-thinking that goes with it. But once Abby was out, while the doctor stitched up Meg's third-degree tear, I went with the baby to the bassinet, to her first weigh-in, first temperature, heel inking, and first bath. She didn't cry just yet. She peed on the doctor in an arc impressive for any girl. Then she hiccuped. And throughout all of this, her gooey little fingers held one of mine.

Too schmaltzy? That's all I've got. The smell of her dirty with blood. The swoop of eyelashes. The tiny spasms in her throat and how when I blew lightly over her face, they stopped long enough for her to purse her lips and flutter her eyes. It didn't seem so hard then, or different, than any morning a man wakes up and truly is a father. I figured choosing it was about the same as it choosing me. There wasn't going to be a phone call to the other guy—because Meg swore Abigail was mine and because, I suspect, she didn't know his last name or number. We'd had a rough patch, that's all. No matter, while the doctor stitched up Meg, I chose.

Abby's sixteen now and almost disappeared from our lives entirely. Meg and I haven't seen Abby, actually *seen* her for days and days.

ONCE IT'S GONE

———————

Peering down into the grill, Noreen shrieks.

"What is it?" calls Meg. She looks back, says, "Be nice, Will," and we walk the rest of the way up the drive.

"I believe it's ruined," says Noreen.

Meatloaf. On the grill. Which, of course, has fallen apart in eggy glops down through the rack. She pinches the tongs together and slips them through one of the side holes in the grate.

"Watch it," I tell her as she scoops bits out of the coals and packs them together on a be-ketchupped platter. "That for the cats?" I say.

She holds out her arm where one slim stripe of flesh is pinking up. "Look here," she says. "Damn it to hell."

"Can we get you some ice for that?" I offer, though it's not much of a burn at all.

"Noreen, your fingers!" says Meg, and sure enough, they're all pricked and scratched, both scabbed over and freshly raw.

She pulls back her hand, tucking it into the bitty front pocket of her apron. "The kitties are a bit shy," she says, shaking us off and heading for the kitchen only to return a minute later with tuna chunked in a heap, the new centerpiece of her ketchup moat.

"You shouldn't be feeding them," says Meg. "They'll just keep coming around. They'll grow to depend on you."

"It keeps them out of the trash," she says, and from the way she's positioning a sprig of mint she's torn off the bush at her side door, I see this really is for the cats and she's making quite a production out of it.

"Noreen," I say. "Seriously, you're not keeping them out of anything. They prowl around every night."

She's walking down to the end of her driveway and we follow her. "There," she says, setting the platter in a spot of grass already mashed down. "We'll have meatloaf another time."

"They probably prefer tuna," says Meg.

"She shouldn't do this," I say to my wife but there's no point in repeating it. We leave Noreen and head home. The corner lamppost flickers and I mark it, intend to call the city on Noreen's behalf. "Do you think she's all right?"

"She'll be okay," says Meg.

We keep walking and I can feel her heartbeat in my hand: a little quiet but steady. Please don't dislike her. She broke my heart but maybe that's not the end of the world we all think it is.

We reach home, the walkway, our door, the dog—aforementioned pacing collie, slowed by her nap and hip dysplasia—comes head low, wagging and blinky. Winnie's old now, too, and the vet says no more long walks or her hips will give out for sure so we either sneak out when she's sleeping or pretend we're getting in the car. But I think she knows. She presses her head against my knees and I rub her bony neck.

Abby hasn't come home yet. Meg's gaze falls to the bowl by

the back door where we all toss our keys. I don't say anything. Abby's coming off a breakup with a boy we all liked. Meg says give her space, so we're officially giving her space by letting her come and go as she pleases.

We begin our nightly rhythms: Meg tidies the kitchen while I open the freezer and deliberate over what to thaw for tomorrow's supper. We head to the bathroom where I strip and Meg leans over the counter to study her face in the mirror. She touches her left cheek, touches it again. She's unhappy with something there, the beginnings of a new spot maybe. I squeeze in beside her, take the toothpaste and my brush, give her hip a nudge with my own. "It's nothing," I tell her, "a freckle, maybe," but she goes on touching that same place on her cheek

Finally, she flosses, smiling while she drags the thread down and back up around each tooth. It's a practice thing she does, smiling, to keep her face from becoming a natural frown. I go for a good long piss and look at her, at the side seams of her panties, the silky strap of her camisole slid down one shoulder, and I want to touch her back. Just that, her back. Not to interrupt her progress from top molars to lower bicuspids. Not to get a kiss out of her or start something sexy or deep. Just to brush her skin and know she is there despite where she went all those years ago with Abby's father.

I go to bed, lie there still and drifting.

"Wake up."

"Is she home?" I say, lurching out of sleep.

"There was a note. She's staying over at Samantha's." Meg pulls the covers off of me. "Come on."

Winnie noses around us to be first out the back door, but Meg takes her by the collar and sends her back inside. She leads me to the garden wall where spent clematis vines are twiggy and full of the pin oak's crisp leaves. Meg points. "Up there," she says. "Hear it?"

I don't, whatever it is. The night's quieter than breathing.

She drags over a patio chair. Where there isn't any bird shit, it's yellow with pollen.

"What?" I ask. Though the air is just shy of too warm, we stand clutching our sleep clothes closed at the neck, whispering in just the barest glow of light from the back porch that reaches around the side of the house here. It feels like a secret.

Meg uses my shoulder to get herself up onto the chair. Then I hold her hips while she rummages around in the vines.

"Meg," I say. "Be careful. What are we doing?"

"Shh."

Then I hear it. A quiet chirp, raspy and trailing.

"There," she says.

"Yeah."

"It shouldn't be cheeping at night," she whispers. "At night is bad. At night means mom's gone, dad's gone, and nobody's coming back." She turns around with the nest in her hands.

She says, "Probably the cats—"

"Of course it was the cats."

"What should we do?" I say.

"We don't leave it to die."

"What if its parents come back?"

"They're not coming back," she says. "Only the cats will be back."

"The shelter's closed now. What time is it do you think?"

Meg has saved birds before, and I know that's what she's thinking of. There was a mourning dove with an eyeball hanging right out of its socket. A neighbor cat attacked it and Meg tried to chase off the cat by screaming at it. When that did nothing but get the cat to flick its ear over and over at her, she scruffed the cat and hurled it in the air. Then she scooped up the bird in a towel and drove to the Humane Society with the bird on her lap. They put it down the second she handed it over and they saw the eye. But humane death was still a saving and Meg felt better even if she threw up all afternoon.

I try to reason with her tonight. "Why don't we just situate the nest back against the trellis, safe at the back, and we can come get it in the morning? That's the best thing, right? Aren't they always saying that about wildlife: Don't move it unless you have to?"

Her eyebrows bunch and her mouth pinches up like a tantrumming two-year-old. She shelters the nest against her stomach.

That's when the cats come. Or maybe they've been here in the bushes watching. They don't wrap around my legs or even the legs of the patio table. They aren't that kind of cat anymore.

Their spines are constant bell curves, the fur at their shoulder blades is practically moussed, that's how spiky it is. They hiss and their mouths stay open to show their teeth. I would jump up on another chair if they weren't so pathetic looking without their fourth legs (and tail). They've all acclimated pretty well to their amputations—all but one of which was caused by being hit by a car back when they were pets. There are rumors about the fourth and what the Dillman kid did or didn't do to his own cat with a lighter and some chewing gum. No one in the neighborhood recognizes or knows what happened to the tabby without its tail, but watch the cats a while and you'll see him lick and nibble that stump so long you come out the other end pretty certain he ate it himself.

"Do something," says Meg, kicking her bare toes at that tailless one standing on its two hind feet to get a better sniff of what Meg is holding. I swear I see the cat lick his lips. I go for the door, let Winnie out, but she barrels through me and limps right past Meg and the cats.

"Jesus, Meg, I don't know," I say, my allergy already kicking in. I sneeze twice and want to rub my eyes. "Can't you just put down the nest? Put down the nest! Or throw it maybe!"

"How can you say that?" The bird chirps again, right on cue.

The white cat without a front paw jumps up on the table. He starts rocking back and forth the way cats do just before a big pounce.

"Will, get some tuna or something!"

"We don't eat tuna," I say, fully aware of how stupid it sounds. "I'll find something."

Inside, I open the cheese drawer of the fridge. We have salami but that doesn't seem right. Dogs love cat food, so I get Winnie's kibble. That's not right either, though. I keep grabbing really stupid boxes or cans of things so that by the time I notice light coming from underneath Abby's door, I have quite a collection of idiotic jars of olives and bread crumbs on the counter.

I knock. "It's Dad. You still up?"

"I don't want to talk about it," she says.

"I need to ask you something."

She doesn't answer, which is teenager for *all right, fine.*

"Abby," I say, putting my hand to the knob.

"I'm not opening the door."

"Mom's out back," I tell her. "There's a bird and those cats. Don't go out there, okay?"

She only sighs.

"I need the broom," I tell her. "I can't find it."

She opens the door but hides behind it. Out comes the broom.

I take a second longer than necessary here with her arm. I haven't seen it in a while. Meg says things are fine but Abby goes out swimming or out with friends or at a movie every night and all day long. She doesn't eat with us. She doesn't talk to us. And she's doing just fine. When I ask Meg about it, she just says, "I hated my mother for all of high school, all of college, and then some," and that's that. Okay, so Abby has reached the stage of hating her mother. But why am I implicated in that? And why hate Meg, who has made every decision pertaining to Abby solely on the reverse basis of what her own mother would have done? And then she not only does the opposite but does it double. Like when Abby wanted to see Panic! At the Disco play Cleveland on a school night, Meg not only said yes, but made her and her friends a hotel reservation and gave her thirty-five dollars to help with gas. And when Abby was fourteen and said she'd had enough of the color purple, which was part of a larger patriarchal oppression as a gender-preapproved color for girls, Meg not only replaced all the towels in the hall bath with baby blue, she also donated her best purple wraparound skirt to Goodwill. That's Meg: everything her mother was not, so that Abby would never hate her the way Meg grew up hating her own mother—and for nothing really. It's inevitable, I guess, no matter what a mother does.

That's what the *Cosmo* in my dentist's waiting room says. I've been having a lot of work done and spent several mornings this week taking the quizzes and reading mother-daughter squabble articles while waiting for the novocaine to kick in.

So Meg thinks things are fine and I can't really tell her otherwise, but standing here outside Abby's door, seeing her thin arm and the delicate knob of wrist bone, I touch her hand, say, "We can talk anytime. I'm your dad."

I take the broom and head back out to save Meg from the

drooling, circling kitties. The littler two scare off right away when I wave the broom. Then the white one and a calico dart when I slam the broom on the flagstone. But the tailless one is actually up on the chair, standing against Meg, reaching up for the nest.

"I kept kicking but it didn't matter," she whispers, holding perfectly still. The nest is safe beneath her chin.

I swing the broom hard, and the cat *rowl*s and hisses but it falls off Meg's thigh, off the chair, and when Winnie comes back around the corner of the house and gives a big, deep woof, the tailless cat finally slinks off.

"That was something," I say, helping Meg down from the chair.

She wipes her eyes one by one. "Wish you'd come with the broom sooner."

"It's okay. You're okay."

"I don't care about me—but it was almost up to the nest. I didn't know what I'd do then."

"I know, I'm sorry."

"At least I saved it."

"Abby's home. I got sidetracked," I say, putting an arm around her. I can see the bird now, featherless and leathery, a head (all beak and eyeballs) bobbles whenever it tries to move. "What now?"

"Shoebox."

I follow Meg inside, watch the nest when she sets it on our

bed. She rummages in the closet. Birds have rare bird diseases they like to give humans, right?

"Here," she says, pulling out the fancy heels and tissue. She hasn't worn those in years. "I wish we had something to feed it. I'll take it to the shelter in the morning." Meg unballs two pairs of my sweat socks and cozies each around the nest to hold it steady. "You mind?" she says, glancing up. The bird's beak snags on a twig of the nest and the head lolls a bit.

"By all means." I don't want to get back in bed yet. It's strange falling asleep when no one else is. I pick up the "Life" section of the paper I didn't read this morning because I was finishing "Big Breakups and the Lonely Girl" in the *Cosmo* I brought home after my crowns were done. I am an expert now on the importance of throwing oneself back into neglected friendships and job. I suppose the advice is universal: teenaged girl, single working woman, middle-aged man living with his wife and the daughter he used to fail to recognize among the crowd of other people's children pouring out of school when he went to pick her up. Now she drives herself.

––––––––––––––

Winnie gets us up at her usual 6:15. I follow her down the hall like a blind person might, both my arms out at my sides, touching the walls to be sure. When I get to Abby's room, I expect it to be empty and the door open. It's not. I stop and listen for her. "Abby?"

The door opens. "I can't tell Mom," she says.

I nod.

She's been crying. Her face shines sticky and tight. Her hair is tangled.

"Abigail," I say. She is breaking my heart.

She hands me a brochure rough and billowed by tears. Same sad teen silhouetted in a window seat as the brochures for all parental nightmares: drug use, suicide, STDs. But this girl has a hand on her stomach, so of course it's the clinic on Twelfth Street. This is really happening.

"You have an appointment here?" I ask my daughter.

She shakes her head. "I already went."

I don't quite know how to express what I feel, the weight of losing what didn't exist ten minutes ago—not to me anyway. And how can nothingness feel like the world? But it does.

I reach out and hold her, stroke her hair and when she must finally be done feeling little and afraid, she says she wants to go to a friend's and Meg has already left for the shelter, so I watch Abby back down the driveway in the Corolla Meg bought her last year.

I go walking along Pitt Street. Hips be damned, Winnie comes too. We take each side street up and back on the way, but inevitably arrive at Noreen's front porch. It's early, she has no reason to be up, so I wait on the swing. And after sniffing out the yard, Winnie comes and lies with her snout on my feet.

The morning is cool, the sun's not yet a part of the air.

Cottonwood seeds come drifting down like summer snow. I think about the cats and where they go in the daytime. I think of Meg up on the chair, cradling the nest against her body, kicking away the nose of the tailless cat. I love her. Even if I think more about touching her than I actually do, I still know what her skin feels like, I still know her spotted cheek against my chest, the way she sometimes goes giddy at night, in bed, when I want to sleep and she wants, not to talk really but, well, I don't know. I never have figured out what it is she wants then. Just some form of closeness, some little noisy wordlessness like when you're first with someone and nobody knows who you are and you don't know who they are and all you want is to eat up that other person and every single little thing they do.

Cosmo says you never get that back with someone once it's gone.

Maybe that's what she wanted from me. Maybe that's what she went looking for way back when. And maybe she found it. I used to be afraid in the nighttime that she was dreaming of that man.

"Will," says Noreen. She's bending for the newspaper when she sees me here on her swing.

Winnie manages to get upright without bending her back legs. It's an ordeal every time and I hate it, but tell her, "Stay."

"I'll make Crystal Light," says Noreen. "It's peach iced tea. Delicious."

I wait at the dining table now, watching her move in the kitchen. In the past five years, Meg's body has become her mother's and what must be nearly every mother's, for it's just like this old woman's: small waist, a swollen lower belly—what Meg calls "the front butt"—and a little extra skin that creases at the base of her neck.

"Stop, okay?" I say, "Please."

She doesn't hear me or doesn't care, so I let her go on with the Tupperware pitcher, ice cubes, and powder scoops.

Finally, Noreen comes to sit. "Is it Meg?" she says because there was a day like this, Abby's lifetime ago, when I came here to Noreen and told her I was leaving. Why, I don't know, but she'd said I was right to go but insisted I tell Meg myself at the hospital. She knew what she was doing. We haven't talked like that since and I wonder if she even remembers and mostly have hoped she doesn't. "She loves you," says Noreen. "You know that."

"I think Abby's had an abortion," I say.

She doesn't speak, just puts a hand over mine.

"I know she has," I say.

"Is she all right?"

"Abby told me," I say. "There's a brochure. She was crying."

"Dear."

"There was a boy she liked. His name was Adam."

"I met him once," she says.

"Okay, right," I say, though I can't imagine how she could have. "Abby told Meg he broke up with her. A while ago. She thinks he was gay."

"Boys change their minds. You tell her that."

"She did things in front of him, all sorts of things—things Meg wouldn't even tell me—and nothing, this boy did nothing."

"Then there's somebody new. He'll be nice. Trust Abby. You need to trust her."

"And then he moved to Fort Worth. So it's not him. It's someone else, Noreen. Someone we've never even met or seen and probably never will now."

"She's taken care of this. Trust your girl." She stirs her glass and watches the golden water move.

"Who even knows who it is," I say.

She's quiet.

"It doesn't matter to her, I guess." I push my glass at this woman. "And that's the thing. It doesn't seem to matter to anyone. Who they screw, who they don't."

"Oh, Will," she says, squeezing my hands. "Don't mix things up."

"I don't understand them! I don't know how it is they feel love and loyalty in all the wrong places." Meg's off saving a goddamned baby bird while Abby goes and kills one.

"Go home, Will. Tell Abby to come home." She peels back a bandage on the tip of her thumb, checking on the cat scratches, then presses it back into the adhesive. "This is *her* sadness," she says. "Let it be hers."

I see the dishes piled high in the kitchen behind her. For such a little woman, these must be a week's worth. I hadn't noticed a smell, and still don't, but I cover my nose and mouth.

"It doesn't mean anything to me, does it?" I say. "Not a damn bit. And that's the trouble: Where am I in any of this?"

Noreen drops her spoon into the glass. "You're a little beside the point," she says, "but you knew that going in."

———————————

It's early evening when Meg walks into the bedroom with the shoebox full of socks. "They put it down," she says. "It was hardly moving by the time I got there. They should be open twenty-four hours. They shouldn't let something die like that just because they're not open. How hard would it be to have each member of the staff sleep there once a week? Just think how many boxes of puppies wouldn't get left out by the train tracks and sacks of kittens drowned off Presque Isle."

She takes my socks out of the box and tosses them in the trash. "You don't mind, do you?"

"Okay."

She picks up the high-heeled shoes and instead of putting them back in the box, she drops them in the trash, too.

"It was just a tiny little bird, Will." She sits, puts her head on my shoulder and I stroke her hair a moment. "What are you doing?"

My gym duffel bag is on the bed next to me. "Thinking," I say.

"If I see those cats," she says, "next time I do, I'm going to do something. Why can't Winnie be a rottweiler? I'd let her roam at night, let her teach those cats a lesson."

Abby doesn't come home until late tonight. Meg is downstairs folding laundry. I am picking leaf bits out of the socks she threw away and placing them in my duffel.

"Everything's okay," says Abby from the doorway. "You didn't say anything, did you, to Mom?"

"Do you feel all right?" I move her long hair out of her eyes, tuck it behind an ear and she tilts her head: half nod, half *stop touching me*. "Was it Adam's?" I ask and she wails, "God!" and storms off.

Meg comes up with a basket of clothes and while we both move around the bedroom putting away shirts and underpants and jeans, I tell her that our daughter had been a mother but isn't anymore, that I don't know what I'm feeling but it is strange and I need some time away, that I will help out with support or whatever she needs. I tell her that nothing—not Meg's heart, not our girl Abigail, and not the little bit of cells I'm mourning—nothing here has ever really been mine. She nods, there isn't anything more either one of us can say.

I wait until the cats come back before picking up my bag. They are out there in the trash cans, knocking down lids and scavenging the neighbors' leftovers. I imagine the shredding of plastic bags, the sucking hiss of them licking their teeth and noses. Winnie's ears prick when an aluminum lid hits the pavement with a shiny gong. But the Westies and dachshunds and Airedale don't answer.

Meg has begun sorting through the dresser drawers for

clothing of mine to donate: spotted shorts from a ChapStick gone through the wash, yoga pants worn through at the knees. The bed is lumps of colored cloth, of linen detritus, and now she opens the closet door to start in on shoes.

"Aren't you going to talk to her?" I say.

"She'll talk when she's ready to talk," says Meg, coming back to the bed to pick up a T-shirt. She refolds it against her chest. She's thought better of tossing this blue shirt, which I recognize as something Abby sometimes borrows. Meg smooths it back into the drawer then sits on the other side of the bed petting Winnie's snout.

Her body. She's given it to no one but me all these years since Abby's birth, I'm certain. But she's hardly given it over to me. Truly given it. And I don't know that I would have taken it. No, I know I wouldn't have at first. But when Abby was three or seven or twelve, yes. Yes, Meg was all I ever thought of. Her lips and tongue the only mouth I wanted on my skin. Space crept in. Space she introduced and space I was scared to cross because doing so would acknowledge the divide.

Winnie agitates. I am putting on shoes and she hobble-stands, twisting Meg's fingers in the collar. "Ouch, you," says Meg.

"Is it possible you're in shock?"

"I thought you were pro-choice," she says. We've always ridiculed the pretend fetus graveyard out on the edge of town. The yellow ribbons and bloody billboard pictures.

"That doesn't mean anything."

"Well, I guess not," she sneers.

"I mean, when it's yours," I say, wondering if there were a blank Abby could have initialed to receive a bag of ashes. "It can still hurt, okay?"

She scratches Winnie behind the ear in an effort to distract her, but the dog shakes her head so Meg just takes her by the collar again. As simply as correcting one of her fifth grader's fractions over his shoulder, she says, "It was *hers.*"

"It was your first grandchild. It could have been ours."

She lets go of Winnie now and takes the duffel from my hands. "Go outside with me," she says.

Have you ever just known, suddenly known, that you are no longer bound to someone's heart? But you want to be, and so you pretend.

For seventeen years.

What's one night more?

Meg's voice is shimmery clear. I touch her side, her shoulder. Feel my fingertips almost pinch her for how I'm trying to hold on.

I am not the most tender husband. I could have kissed her bare shoulders last night in the bathroom, after all. Instead, I fell asleep *thinking* of action. But I'd like to think I'm a good husband, someone who genuinely loves his wife and would do anything for her.

This morning, before I saw Abby, before Meg failed to save the bird, we bumbled into each other moving from toilet to sink to shower. We dressed quietly. I grabbed a pair of navy shorts and Meg's fingers brushed the hem of a green shirt hanging in the closet to let me know what matched. She had missed the top clasp of the band of her bra but I didn't say anything and I didn't fasten it or touch her. I watched her blouse fall down her back.

"You remind me of the cats right now," she had said, swigging a Dixie cup of water from the bathroom tap. "The way you're watching me."

I curled one arm and pretended to limp a circle around her. I stood still behind her back and that time I did touch her, the shallow gully of her lower back.

"We should talk," I said.

"Yes," she said. "Later." She was dressed then, had the shoebox and bobblehead bird clutched tight. "Tonight."

Standing here now with my reclaimed duffel and my wife, I cannot for the life of me recall what it was I would have said to her, nor decipher her "yes." What had she known?

"Please," says Meg, tugging me down the hall. "Come lie down in the grass and let me tell you I wish I could undo things."

She never has. Not ever. And maybe that can be the key.

She touches my face and her hands are wet. "Before you leave," she says.

So I am going. I am finally going.

I take my hands from hers but follow her, move down the hallway, separate. We stop outside Abby's door and although it is late, there is light. I think maybe to ask for the broom again, to see her arm and maybe hold her close enough I can smell Meg's blood in her hair. Tell the little lie again.

The dog's caught up to us by now. Meg bends down, whispers, "You can't go, Winnie. No one can go. Will," she says. She stands back up. "It was never about you. It was nothing you did or didn't do. It was just something stupid except that there's Abby but that's it. You know. Truly, deep down you know it was nothing."

"This is ours," she says. "This house. This dog. This life. The garden. Our walks and our suppers. How we talk quietly in bed before we've even woken up. That's all ours." Her eyes are wet but hold back everything, even her voice remains steady, reasonable.

I take Meg's hands, look at them and at the glint of dark night in her eyes. I set her fingers around Abby's doorknob, squeeze them tight there. "Talk to her," I say. "This is yours."

I step outside and the night is heavy with tomorrow's rain. They've forecasted morning thunder but no one on the block has listened. The cans are ready, neatly standing at the edge of every driveway. Nothing ever looks so civilized as a dark street waiting for next-day trash pickup, and nothing so uncivilized as the sag of rain-soaked cardboard boxes and wadded Kleenex glued to a wet street. I reach for our cans, drag them to the road and see around the bend, Noreen surrounded by the cats. She's carrying a salad bowl full of something they want down to the curb and they're swishing circles and running ahead of her. She sets down the bowl and the tailless tabby begins eating first. He takes a bite then shakes the food to the back of his mouth. The white cat eats, too, then the smaller one, and now they're all eating together. And Noreen, who does not see me, is speaking to them. I can't hear her words, but her lips move in soft shapes. She kneels behind the cats and begins stroking their backs, which arch, but they do not stop eating.

I don't wait to see the tailless one scratch her or the calico pounce on her knobby hand and hold it there like a stunned mole, immobile, a few seconds before letting go. I don't stay to see her scared to cry out for fear of chasing them away. Or the look across her face when they leave the bowl clean and she takes it in to wash. I walk back up the driveway, to my own life, my own house of cats.

We are all hungry.

Sick Days

When **Mom is** out sick from work, she bakes trays of brownies for Sean and me. And a whole one for herself. She plans things the night before and comes home with a party-size bag of Cheetos, a pack of Twizzlers, and a box of Entenmann's donuts. She'll give us money, say, "Order two pizzas. You know what I like."

She does her eating in her room, in her bed. She doesn't want to be seen. When the pizzas come, we knock and leave hers outside her door. No plate, nothing. A minute later, the box is gone. Sean says she goes feral on her eating days. I don't disagree. Once I caught sight of her leaving the empty pizza box outside her door. She wasn't dressed, just rolled in a fitted sheet, one of its corners wrapped over her forehead, the elastic biting a jagged pink moon into her skin.

All the rest of the days in the year, she diets. Eats just 750 calories a day. And I know you won't believe that number. But her metabolism is messed up, okay? She's been little and huge and little and huge a billion different times in her life, and if she eats more than 750 calories a day, she gains weight. So that's what she eats and she weighs every gram of food, usually. And she gets these pills, Adderall and Topamax, from her psychiatrist to push her weight loss along because she's still 240 pounds. And it's working, last year she was 337. But the sick days. They scare us.

Today is Saturday and she's supposed to be at her drive-up teller window with the pneumatic tube sending people's deposit and withdrawal slips back and forth all day, but she's in her room and we're in the living room, lying on the carpet with Foster, our dog. He's white and brown because he's mostly a Jack Russell but also kind of a pit bull, so he's bigger and taller than a Jack Russell and smaller and shorter than a pit. Whatever you think he is, basically, he's wrong.

"We should do something," says Sean, rubbing Foster's belly.

"Like what?"

He sits up. "Maybe if we curled her hair." He touches his own short hair between two straight fingers like to curl it.

"She doesn't want her hair curled," I tell him.

"Maybe she does. You don't know everything, Amelia." He's back to stroking Foster again and again in the same spot so that a collection of shed white fur piles up. I watch him to see what he's going to do with it.

"Let's go out," I tell him.

Sean shakes his head. "We could brush her hair." He picks a bit of the pile of loose fur off Foster and sprinkles it down to the carpet.

"Don't do that," I say.

He shrugs. "That's where it all goes anyway."

"You could put it in the trash," I say.

He lies back down and Foster goes over to his bed and curls up, his little tail wagging as he lies down. Sean is nine and I'm twelve. He's probably going to be trans one day if he ever gets up enough courage.

"Do you hear that?" says Sean.

It's Mom.

We go sit in the hallway outside her door. Foster follows us, though we have to pull him back because he's panting and trying to sit against her door and we don't want her to hear him. She's talking to her computer men. All giddy now because that's how she gets. She just talks to new men on different sick days and then never talks to them again.

We hear her laugh. We can't make out the words she says. Just laughing and her voice is higher with them. Sometimes she says *No* but she doesn't say it the same as when she says it to us. It's like a *Yes*. It's a *Yes-No*. She moves around the room, walking while she talks, I guess. I picture her still in the fitted sheet, the elastic biting her forehead, and I shove my fist in my mouth to stop the giggle. Sean gives me a death glare and Foster starts to lick my cheek. I turn away from his slobber. Mom's saying *No* and laughing some more but then she must hang up because the house goes silent except for our breathing and Foster now licking my knees.

Sean and I don't move. We side-glance our eyes to each other but we do not move. She won't come out, right? She wouldn't come out. Not until tomorrow.

"Hel-lo," we hear.

Thank the baby Jesus. Oh my God. I thought we were going to die.

And she's laughing and there are *No*s and *Yes-No*s and more laughing. Foster lies down. Sean lies down. My knees are slimy. I get up and go to my room, grab my jacket, and head outside.

It's November and the air is cold on my wet knees. I walk to Chrissy's building, go to her door.

"Want to come out?" I ask.

"Where's Sean?" she says.

"He's too young for you."

"Oh my God, Amelia!"

"Kidding!" I say. "He's back at home, staking out my mom's door."

"Why?"

"She's sick."

"Oh." She runs a cherry ChapStick over her lips and holds it out to me.

I shake my head. "Come on," I say.

We walk to the playground equipment by the parking lot. Chrissy sits on a swing and I sit on one next to her.

"What were you doing?" I ask.

"Nothing," she says. "YouTube."

I walk my swing back to push off but just stand there for a minute, waiting.

"You?" she says, she walks her swing back, too, then pushes off and is in the air.

"Nothing." I let myself go and I'm in the air now, too. Both of us pumping to stay up, go higher.

"Exciting lives we lead," shouts Chrissy, laughing into the wind we're making.

"Totally."

Chrissy is a tad bit pudgy. I don't know if she knows, but yeah, I guess she does. She doesn't act like my mom, though. She doesn't go nuts with restricting calories and she doesn't go nuts with indulging in calories. Mostly, she doesn't go nuts. But in school, she doesn't get called on for dodgeball teams until it's the special needs kids. And she didn't get a role in the class play when everyone got a role in the class play; instead, she was made stage manager. At the end of a school year, teachers and parents always say get ready for the next year, it's a big step up in maturity. But sixth grade is when everyone decided to care about superficiality so now there's a boy, Wayne Moten, that calls Chrissy Lane, Chubby Lane. In fifth grade, he was her boyfriend and she was just as pudgy. And on "Meet the Teacher" night, when my mom signed up to bring cookies for a bake sale, Gordon Riley saw her name is Marjorie and now asks me every day, "How's Marge the Barge?"

Sean and Foster come running up now. "She came out!" he yells. I pump my legs and he backs up out of the way of my swing.

"What?"

He's breathless. "She came out!"

I stop pumping. I reverse pump. "She's out?"

Sean nods.

Chrissy stops pumping. She slows down.

I jump off in midair. I walk away from the swings because I don't want Chrissy to hear. "What did she say? What did she do? Was she in the sheet?"

Sean says, "She had a dress on and said she's going out."

"Going out," I repeat.

"On a date," he says.

"A date?" It's Chrissy. She's come up behind me now and is scratching Foster behind his ears.

"How can she go on a date?" I ask. "I mean, she doesn't even know any of these men. They could be ax murderers."

Sean says, "They could follow her home, tie us all up, and make us watch *Wheel of Fortune* while they force-feed us cubes of green Jell-O."

"You are so weird, Sean," says Chrissy.

He smiles and Foster wanders over to the slide.

"We should go home," I say. "See you later, Chrissy."

Foster's pooping by the slide now. We're supposed to pick it up, but I don't have any bags so we pretend we don't see him.

When we get home, Mom is playing her old Depeche Mode and Yaz tapes and getting ready for her date. Going down the hall to her room, we can smell the curling iron heating and Sean says, "See? She did want it." He runs into her bathroom and offers to curl her hair and she sits on the toilet and lets him. He's actually really good at it. Mom has long, light brown hair like mine but hers will hold a curl really nice. I got my dad's fine, straight hair.

Foster uses the stairs to get up on Mom's super-high bed and I sit on the bed, too. I listen to Mom and Sean. They don't talk much but they make soft sounds particular to each of them—Sean's are high-pitched oohs and Mom's are low thrums—and all of a sudden, I feel homesick for each of them and both of them together, even though they're right there. I know it doesn't make any sense but my heart aches like I'm a million miles away.

"Ta-da!" says Mom, stepping out of the bathroom and spinning around to show off her hair. "What do you think?"

"Really nice," I say. "Beautiful."

"Are you okay?" She touches my cheek and looks into my eyes.

I blink a few times.

"What is it, Melie?" she says.

"I don't know."

She hugs me and holds me and that feels right. But now Sean has to come get in between us because he likes to be the peanut butter.

"How about Amelia helps me pick what to wear tonight," Mom says.

"Okay," I say.

"But I'm better at that," says Sean.

"Be nice," she tells him. "Besides, you got to do my hair." Mom goes to her closet and starts moving hangers from right to left one by one.

Sean lies down on the bed next to Foster, says, "Fine, we'll just be over here not helping you look your best, right Foster?"

"Don't be a butthead, Sean," I say. I go stand with Mom. "Do you know where you're going?"

"To an Italian restaurant for dinner."

"Okay, so something a little bit nice but not *too* dressy." I pull out a white collar shirt, some skinny jeans, a wide black belt, and her black suede boots. "Good?"

"Great job. What do you think, Seany?"

He lazily lifts his head from the bed and sighs. "It will have to do."

I go to her jewelry box and pick out an amethyst geode necklace and some amethyst threader earrings while Mom gets dressed.

We go out to the living room and wait. Sean rolls around on the carpet with Foster. I sit on the sofa. Mom stands.

"When is he coming?" I ask.

"Forty minutes." She checks her watch for the millionth time.

"Well, you may as well sit down."

"Sit down here with me," says Sean. "Foster wants you." Foster wags his stumpy tail.

"She doesn't want to get dog fur all over her date clothes," I say.

"That's true," says Mom. "Sorry, Sean." She goes to the windows like maybe she'll see him walking up the path right now.

"Do you even know what this guy looks like?" says Sean.

Mom doesn't turn around. "Yes, from his picture."

"If that's really him," Sean says.

"True," she says.

"What picture did you use?" I ask.

"Uh, well—"

"I mean, is it a current picture or, like, an out-of-date picture?"

She turns back to me now and I feel accused. "You mean do I have this body or a slimmer body in it? Am I dishonest about my current physique?"

I feel bad for asking now. What does it matter? She's still the same person, isn't she? Well, except that now she eats obsessively little most of the time, other than sick days. So maybe she's not the same person now but not in the way those men will think.

"Are you nervous?" I ask.

She nods.

Finally she sits on the couch and we watch some of a Jim Gaffigan comedy special. There are too many self-deprecating fat jokes and Mom laughs at them but they aren't funny, they're just mean. I think about Chrissy and text her not to watch it. She answers "Why?" and I don't know what to say so I don't answer.

The doorbell rings and Foster goes crazy barking. He runs to the door. Mom jumps up and tells Sean to get the dog. I get up, too, and we're all standing there in the entryway when she opens the door to the guy.

Mom says, "You must be Kirk. Come in and meet everybody."

"Hi. Hey," he says. He's all right looking. He has wavy hair and he's kind of short, shorter than Mom, but his face is cute like a baby's with a really good smile.

"This is Amelia," says Mom.

"Hi," I say.

"Hello," he says and shakes my hand.

"And this is Sean," she says.

"Hi," says Kirk and shakes Sean's hand.

"And this is Foster," says Sean.

Foster's quiet now and sitting between Sean's feet.

"He's a real cutie," Kirk says, "will he mind if I pet him?"

Sean says, "Go on."

Kirk strokes the top of Foster's head and scratches his neck. Foster gets that far-off look in his eyes.

Mom takes me aside. "The instructions for the lasagna are on the counter. I'll be home by 10, 10:30 at the latest." She looks at Kirk.

"Scout's honor," he says.

"She should have worn a dress," says Sean.

"You should wear a dress," I say.

He disappears. A few minutes later, he comes out in my old summer dress that he loves to wear.

We eat the lasagna and Sean feeds some to Foster. We watch the rest of Jim Gaffigan and wonder what happened because he used to be so funny. We roll around on the carpet with Foster. We watch stupid TV and then Sean falls asleep and I get my book and I must fall asleep reading because the next thing I know, Mom is here and Kirk is here, too, and Mom is telling Kirk Sean's dress is for practicing a role in a play and then she is carrying Sean to bed. Then they come back for me and I get up and go to bed and Mom follows me and leans over me and whispers, "You had to let him wear the dress tonight?" and I feel sick.

———————————

In the morning, Mom is whistling and mopping the kitchen. She calls out to me, "Good morning, Sunshine."

"Morning," I say.

"Sleep well?"

"Yeah."

"Seany's still sleeping."

"Oh," I say. I sit just outside the wet floor on the carpet. Foster noses under my arm so I'll pet him. He lies down beside me. "Did you have a good time on your date?" I ask.

"Yes, ma'am," she says, running the mop over the same patch of linoleum over and over again.

"Your hair is still curly."

She reaches up and lightly squeezes a couple of the curls. "Your brother does such a good job on it, doesn't he?"

"When will the floor be dry?" I ask.

"A half hour."

"I'm hungry."

"Sorry, Sugar."

"Do you have anything in your room?"

She turns fast to me. "I don't hoard anymore."

"Oh. Okay." Foster is starting to snore so I focus on him. "I guess it's good you went out on a sick day. So you could eat."

"I'm done with sick days and 750-calorie days," she says.

"What are you going to do?"

She stops mopping and smiles at me. "I'm just going to be happy. Kirk says I'm beautiful."

I go crawl in bed with Sean. He's still in my dress. I curl up behind him and Foster jumps up with us, too. He curls up at our feet under the covers.

When I wake it's to water. The spray of Mom in the shower so I get out of Sean's bed and go to the kitchen for something to eat. But she's there. Cutting up strawberries and mixing up batter for pancakes.

"Who's in the shower?" I ask but then I don't need to ask and feel dumb for saying the words.

"Kirk's apartment had the water shut off this morning," she says, "so I told him he could come back over here and use ours."

She stirs the batter more vigorously, which you're not supposed to do. You're supposed to leave some lumps. She stops stirring and looks up at me and smiles.

"Foster didn't bark."

"I guess he's used to Kirk now, plus wasn't Foster in sleeping with you?"

"He would have heard the door. He would have barked," I say.

Mom picks up her stirring spoon and starts waving it at me. "I don't know what you think you know but that's not what's happening here, so stay in your own lane, Missy."

I go get changed and get my jacket and leave for Chrissy's apartment. By the time I get there, I'm seething. "Come out," I say and I pull on her sleeve to yank her out the door.

"Let me get proper dressed," she says so I go in and sit on her bed while she changes. "What's going on?"

"She had the date."

"Was he cute?" says Chrissy.

"Who cares. Not the point," I say. "He's in my apartment right now."

"Oh my God! Go, Marjorie."

"Gross!"

"When do you think is the last time she had sex?"

"I don't."

"But really, I mean, she's a human being. Your dad left when she was pregnant with Sean, right? Has there been anyone since him?"

"Why are you being all realistic and humanistic and kind to her? You're supposed to be grossed out and want to call CPS that some guy she just met last night is in my house right now and, apparently, was the whole night." I go to Chrissy where she's standing at her dresser and put my hands on either side of her head and give her a good shake. "I could have been raped or murdered or raped and murdered!"

"Were you?" she says.

I roll my eyes.

"Maybe he's nice." She sits down on the bed so I sit next to her.

"Maybe he's pretending to be nice."

"Maybe but why?" she says.

"To kill us all in our sleep."

"He could have done that last night but didn't so that's probably off the table."

"I guess."

"What are you really worried about?" Chrissy pops her knuckles.

"I don't know, what does he want from her? Can he really like her?"

"Because she's so big?"

"I'm sorry, Chrissy, it's just that most people don't want someone my mom's size."

"I know." She turns away from me.

We're quiet a minute, then I say, "You're nowhere near that big, anyway." But it doesn't matter. She won't look at me now.

We sit in the silence on her bed for a while.

Finally, I say, "Let's go outside."

"I don't really feel like it today," she says.

"Chrissy, I'm sorry."

"It's okay. It's how you feel. Whatever."

"It's not how *I* feel. I love you. You're my best friend."

"But you wouldn't marry me."

"I'm not gay."

"That's not what I mean!"

"I know."

———————————

At home, Kirk and Mom are giggling over pancakes at the dining table. Foster lies waiting between them, hopeful.

"Get over here, Amelia," she says. She's got real syrup on the table and a big puddle of it on her plate. "Where've you been?" Then to him, she says, "Probably went to see her best friend Chrissy who lives a couple of buildings over that way." She points behind his head.

He nods.

I stand beside her. "Want me to get you the diet syrup?" I ask.

She lays down her fork and looks up at me. "I'm doing just fine, but I thank you."

"Just trying to help," I say.

"Why don't you go wake up Sean and make sure he gets dressed in a shirt and pants today."

"Oh Mom," I say, "is today the day for small minds?"

Kirk looks between us and back to his plate.

"Go, Amelia. Now."

Foster follows me to Sean's room. We both get on the bed. I give Sean a shake that gets progressively more violent until he finally opens his eyes.

"I knew it was you," he says. "I just wanted to see how far you would take it. You took it really far."

"All the way to shaken baby syndrome?" I ask.

"All the way."

"Mom wants you up," I say. "And dressed."

He pops up. "Ta-da!" He does a little curtsy in the dress on top of the bed. Foster sighs and moves down to the end of the bed.

"She said 'shirt and pants,'" I mock her voice and squeeze my nonexistent curls.

Sean doesn't laugh. "But it's the weekend," he says.

"You don't understand. The guy is still here."

"Still?" Sean sticks his finger in his mouth like to puke.

I nod. "They're eating pancakes and—get this: she's eating regular syrup!"

"No way!"

I nod.

"He just stayed all night?"

"She had some line about the shower blah, blah, blah. He definitely was here all night."

"Gross!"

"What's going on in here?" Mom is standing in Sean's doorway. Who knows how much she heard?

"Nothing," we say and Sean sits back down on the bed with me.

Mom comes in. She walks to the bed and puts a hand on each of our heads, like we're still babies. She says, "I know you probably have some questions about Kirk and me and what all this means for us, but I really, really like him and I'm asking—no, I'm begging you to please show him kindness and exert a little self-control. Amelia, please no snarking comments or judging. And Sean, please no dress until he knows you better."

"So we can't be ourselves," I say.

She removes her hands. "Just be your best selves for a little while."

"What does a dress have to do with whether Sean is his best self or not?" I say.

"A lot," says Sean.

"You know what I mean," says Mom. "It can make people," and now she lowers her voice, "especially men, uncomfortable."

I respond loudly: "That sounds like their problem."

"Amelia, God damn it," she says, cutting her eyes at me hard. "This isn't up for debate. No dress." She turns around and leaves.

Sean hugs his legs to his chest and we sit quietly until we hear Mom back in the room with Kirk, laughing hysterically.

That's when Sean loses it. He rolls over in a ball and sobs without a sound and Foster and I wrap ourselves around him and his dress.

For weeks Mom and Kirk are inseparable. He sleeps over most nights and they stop making up pretenses for his early morning presence. They go out to restaurants and bars and bowling and movies. Once they took us with them but we were more uncomfortable than they were—we spent the night talking in Muppet voices—so we doubt they'll ever repeat that.

For their two-month anniversary, Mom bought Kirk a pair of cufflinks, which is stupid because he sells cars at a place where everyone wears red polo shirts with the S. Smeltzer logo on the shirt so he can't wear the cufflinks to work and maybe he'll wear a button-down shirt on a date with her, but one with cufflink holes? No way. Anyway, they're monogrammed with his initials, KRK, but if you look too fast, it kind of looks like KKK so what was she thinking and what were his parents thinking?

Mom is standing at her closet, trying to figure out what to wear tonight. She's had to go backward in her sizes because she's been eating so much and going out so much. She won't tell us how much she's gained but she's gone up three whole sizes. I guess Kirk doesn't care. There's a big difference between size

28 and size 22. There's a big difference in her face now. In the fullness of her cheeks and the invisibility of her chin. Other kids have moms who change their hair color, maybe, the cut, but that's it—the rest of her stays the same. Our mom changes everything about her: her face, her skin, her size, her shape, her movement when she walks, how she sounds when she talks, how she eats, how she thinks about food, what she says to us, how she loves.

She pulls a long black skirt and a black V-neck sweater from the far end of the closet and she dresses inside the bathroom. She chooses her own jewelry, just like she's been curling her hair all this time. We don't offer to help and she doesn't ask. When she's finished readying herself, she turns to us where we are on her bed and asks, "Good enough?"

"Good enough," we say and we all file out of her room.

She's at the dining room table now, moving some of the contents of her regular purse into a smaller purse for tonight.

Sean goes to her. "Mom," he says softly, "two months is a long time."

"I know it is," she says, stopping what she's doing and getting giddy. "I'm so excited."

"So does he know me now?"

"Of course he knows you." She strokes his cheek.

He whispers, "So I can wear my dress now?"

"Oh," she says. "Let's just give it a while longer. Two months isn't all that long for something like that. We'll just give it a while longer."

"Oh," he says.

Sean disappears into his room and I go to follow him.

"Wait, Amelia," says Mom. "I need you to grab Foster when Kirk gets here."

"Can't you?"

"It's easier with two people."

I wait and I hold Foster when Kirk arrives with his bouquet of pink roses that Mom hands to me. So now I'm holding a dog and a bouquet. And with her at the door, I see there's a flat spot on the back of her head where she didn't curl some of her hair. Sean would never have let that go. I smile at that, then feel bad.

"Sean, come say goodnight!" she calls but he doesn't come and she gets impatient so they leave.

I set down her flowers on the kitchen counter, right next to the sink but out of water, and I go to him. "They're gone," I say.

He nods.

"Do you want to watch something?"

He shrugs.

I go in his dresser drawer and get the dress. "I think you should wear this."

"You heard her."

"Who cares?"

"I can't."

"Sure you can."

He shakes his head.

"Do you know, if you wanted, you could wear this dress

everywhere you went? Everywhere. I mean, you could go outside in this dress. You could go to school in this dress. You could go to the grocery store in this dress. You could have a job one day in this dress. You could get married in this dress. You could do anything and everything in this dress."

Sean picks at his cuticles. "I don't think it would still fit me then."

I give him a little shove. "You know what I mean."

"But she says I can't."

"She's a person. You're a person. I'm a person. But you are the person in charge of you. She's not. You get to decide what's right for you. And if it's wearing this dress, then you get to do that."

"But what will she do to me?"

"I don't know, be mad?" I say. "Ground you. You don't go anywhere anyway."

"Hey."

"Will she stop loving me?"

"It's not possible. If she did, if she possibly could, then she didn't really love you in the first place."

He takes off his T-shirt and slips the dress over his head. Now he runs and spins in the living room with Foster, singing, "I Feel Pretty" from his favorite musical he makes us watch all the time. He spins and spins, the skirt of the dress flaring out around him like a tutu. Sean is the happiest I have seen him since Mom and Kirk became inseparable, maybe ever. I take a video and some pictures on my phone. He spins and sings until his legs give out and he collapses in a heap with Foster licking his face and then I take pictures of that, too.

We make the freezer pizza Mom left for us and eat it, watching *Tin Star*. Sean eats his cheese off first, then scrapes the sauce off with his teeth. Then eats the crust. "You know that's weird, right?" I say.

"I know it's delicious," he says.

"Weird."

"Melie." He pauses the show. "Don't let me fall asleep in the dress tonight, okay?"

"How else will they see the real you?"

He takes hold of my arm and shakes it. "Please," he says. "Swear it."

"Okay."

"Swear it," he says.

"I swear."

He tries to look me in the eye.

"Start the show," I say.

I don't purposefully fall asleep.

Or maybe I do. Maybe I've become a liar and a terrible human being no one should trust anymore. We are asleep in the living room when Mom and Kirk walk in, and there's no time to strip Sean out of the dress, and let's face it, would I even if I had enough time? I keep my eyes shut.

Mom steps over to us quietly, then sees what he's wearing. "God damn it," she whispers. Now I hear Kirk, the jingle of his keys, coming closer.

Mom says, "Oh Kirk, he must have been practicing that play again."

"They still haven't finished that yet?" says Kirk.

"I wish they wouldn't have boys dressing like girls," Mom says. "It's so confusing to young kids." She must be giving Sean a little shake to get him walking to bed. "Seany. Sea-ny."

For a while the room is quiet, only it's not completely quiet. Mom is gone and Sean is, too. But without their noise, I start to make out something else: Kirk's breathing. He's sitting somewhere close, but not too close, probably the dining room, and just breathing. And it's an intimate sound and an intimate thing to be hearing and I don't want to be shut in a soundscape with just him but Foster must have gone with Mom and Sean so it's just the two of us. I try to focus on my own breathing and the sound of my heart beating and pumping blood through my ears. It isn't enough.

"Amelia, I need to see you in your room. Now."

My eyes pop open. Could she tell I wasn't asleep? I go sit on my bed and Mom follows. She shuts the door and sits beside me.

"Your brother is heartbroken." There is something green in her teeth.

"Sean, why?"

"Because you told him to wear the dress when he was

forbidden from wearing it and because you *swore* you wouldn't let him fall asleep in it."

"Aren't you glad your son has character?"

"My son is nine years old. I don't think he knows what he has yet."

"You're blind," I say.

"Don't talk to me like that." She shakes when she says it.

"Since when do you not want to see who he is? You used to love all his little differences. Now you shut him down and say he doesn't know who he is? That's crap and you know it."

Her cheeks are red, either from wine or from me. "I said, don't talk to me like that. Show me respect."

"Then deserve it."

She stands up and the bed creaks.

"Why are you changing for some guy?" I say. "Your son isn't a cis boy, don't make him be one."

She leaves. I walk the back hallway and go to Sean. He's not in the dress. I tell him I'm sorry but he's asleep, tears dried across his cheeks, Foster curled up against Sean's belly. I tell him I'm sorry again and again. I squeeze in bed around Foster and fall asleep there, too.

In the morning, I wake alone in Sean's bed. I go get dressed and can hear their voices, the three of them. When I come out, I see they're playing Candy Land and Kirk just fell all the way back to Cookie Commons. Sean is up near Candy Castle so he's happy. Mom is in Lollypop Woods, neither ahead nor behind.

Kirk pats the chair next to him, says, "Come on over. I think next up is Farkle, right Sean?"

I stay standing. "I hate Farkle," I say.

"That's too bad," he says. "Maybe we can vote on Farkle."

"No, I think the lineup's all set," says Mom. "Maybe you can make a suggestion after Farkle."

"It's fine," I say. Sean won't look at me. I go to the kitchen, get a bowl of Crispix and there are her roses, their heads bent and petals mushy.

"Don't make a mess," Mom says. "I just finished cleaning up after our breakfast."

"No problem." I dump the cereal into the trash and put the bowl back into the cupboard. "I don't need any breakfast."

"Amelia, quit it with the attitude, thank you." Mom draws her card and advances to a purple square. "Your turn, Hon."

Kirk takes a card and it must be something good because he whoops and says, "Thank you, thank you, thank you!"

"Um, you're still in last place," says Sean.

"That is true," says Kirk. "But I'm on the move now, I can feel it."

I go stand at their table again and try to get Sean to look at me and he just won't so then I shoot daggers into Mom's eyes and into the side of Kirk's head. I go to my room, and pull all of my old clothes, all my old dresses out of my closet and heap them onto the carpet. I go back to the kitchen.

"What are you doing rummaging around in there?" says Mom.

"Spring cleaning," I say, pulling out a garbage bag from under the sink.

I go back to my room and Foster has made a nest out of the clothing. I pull at each hemline and sleeve to get him off and put each dress in the bag and then I start to cinch it up. But it's not finished. I go to Sean's room. I get my old dress from the very back of one of his dresser drawers, take it back to my room, put it in the bag, and tie up the bag.

I drag the garbage bag to the front hall. Everyone turns to look at what I'm doing.

"What is that?" Mom asks.

"Spring cleaning, I told you," I say.

"No, really, what is it."

"Old clothes to donate." I put my hands on my waist.

"Don't do anything with that before I get a chance to go through it," she says.

"They're my old clothes and they don't fit anymore," I say. "Surely I can dispose of them how I wish."

"Well I bought them, so no, I get to say how we dispose of them."

"God!" I scream and run to my room and slam the door. I feel like I want to throw up, listening to them roll the dice and yell *Farkle*! I do a crossword on my phone for a while but get stumped and then just start writing in angry words everywhere, crossing hatred with fury and wrath, revulsion with murder and loathing, and so on. I fall asleep, I guess, and when I wake up, I hear Sean crying just outside my door and then going down our hall to his room. Mom's voice trails after him.

I stick my head out and see the garbage bag open. He found the dress. Kirk is alone at the dining table. I go and sit at the other end of the table.

"Hey," he says. "You feeling any better?" He's dealing himself a Solitaire game.

I shrug.

We don't say anything for a while. The game boxes are stacked in front of me. Candy Land, Farkle, Sushi Go!, Exploding Kittens, Blokus, and decks of cards.

He moves a king stack to an empty spot. Then he says, "Your mom said you and Sean used to get along so well and with her, too. I kind of wonder if it's my fault for being here that's messed things up for the three of you."

I shrug again.

"Well, if you can think of anything I'm doing wrong, please tell me, okay?" He deals an ace of hearts from his hand and plays its two from his board.

I pull out my phone. I pull up the video. "You really want to know what it is?" I say.

"Of course." He lays down his hand.

I give him my phone, say, "This is who Sean really is. This is what makes him happy. Hit play."

Sean comes to life on the screen, spinning and singing just like Maria.

"He hands the phone back to me. "Does Marjorie know?"

I nod.

"I don't know what to say." He runs his hands through his hair and lets out a deep breath. "It's different."

"No, it's not," I say. "If he were a girl, you wouldn't find it 'different.'"

"But he's a boy. Just give me a sec, okay?"

I look at the first picture after the video, of Sean's elated face.

I go to the kitchen. Kirk packs up his Solitaire game. I make cereal again and take it to the living room.

Eventually, Mom follows Kirk to the door and Sean follows Mom, watching from the open hallway. Mom's crying, saying, "Please don't go."

"I'll call you tomorrow," says Kirk, one hand on the open door. "I just need a little time to think it through is all."

"We can think it through together," she says, her hand holding his other wrist he's twisting to free. "We can make a plan for the family."

"Marjorie, I love you, but we aren't a family just yet. You three are, I'm just an onlooker at this point and it's important for you to be firm with that distinction."

"Please," she says. "Please don't go. I'll throw away the dress."

I look at Sean's face, and, this time, it's stone.

"I won't ever let him wear another dress ever again," she says.

SICK DAYS

"I don't think that's probably the right thing to do," says Kirk. He removes her hand and gently places it at her side. "I'm sorry."

_____

Kirk doesn't call the next day or the next or ever again. Sean puts the dress back in his dresser but he doesn't wear it anymore; one day I go to check on it and it's not there. I stopped asking Chrissy to come out with me because she never will. So it's just Sean and me on the swings with Foster. But there is something gone between us. Something spun out of the way we talk and move and are with each other. Mom calls us *sullen* these days and I guess that's about as good a word as any for us now. But I think maybe *sad* is what Sean is instead.

Today is a sick day so we want to be anywhere but at home where she's gorging on hoarded forbidden foods in her bedroom. We're sitting in the swings but not swinging. We kick our toes at the rocky dugout beneath each swing. I reach out a hand to my brother and it takes a minute for him to notice or to want to hold mine but he does. He reaches back and holds my hand so maybe there is that little bit of something left in a whole lot of nothing.

The Mud Pit

for Kizzy

I t was the summer a flash storm flooded our back alley and all us kids got out our Big Wheels and skidded through the raging current that washed us down our alleyway and out the other end. Into the street if we were lucky, and if we weren't lucky enough to pedal and steer out in time, down into the muddy gulch fifteen feet wide and twenty feet deep on the other side of the road. Someone's dad had tied a rope around a nearby tree trunk there, for the purpose of climbing out, years before all of us were born. No one knew if it would work in a torrential downpour. Until that day. And then we did. Some of us did.

I was nine and this was in Mineola, Texas, where our street shared an inclined alley, that during any normal rainstorm, made a perfect Big Wheels rain regatta for me and the eighteen elementary school kids on our block. But on the day of the flash flood, the oldest and coolest among us, Booth Russell, was on his Green Machine, the first to go screaming down the new and dangerous course. He zoomed down the alley, hydroplaning left and right, then spun out spectacularly into the road, and was washed over the curb and into the gulch in one swift kick of a wave.

The kids still waiting to go, standing at the top of the alley, could only see him disappear. Three of us—Corrine Butcher and Jeb Gordy—had run down there and stood next to the mudhole in our colored plastic ponchos like slick Tic Tacs, watching Booth pant and pick up his Green Machine out of the foot of muddy water and try to throw it all the way up to us.

"You okay?" said Corrine, the rain pounding so hard on her back it sounded like a doctor doing percussion to listen for pneumonia.

Booth didn't hear or chose not to answer. The Green Machine was an extra long Big Wheel and made for an extremely unwieldy item to hoist so high overhead. Plus, he was twenty feet below ground. But he tried. Again and again, he tried, grunting each time he heaved it. It fell back down on him every time, growing heavier with muddy water in the wheels and seat. And each time, I remember thinking he would start yelling like my mom in the kitchen when something burned or I left a sticky drink ring because I didn't use a coaster. But he was quiet.

"Just leave it," I called to him. "Just leave it!"

Booth looked up at me or maybe just into the hot rain blowing. He opened his mouth but remained silent.

"Is he drinking the rain?" said Corrine, pushing matted brown hair back up inside the hood of her blue poncho—the blue so pretty, it matched her eyes. I slipped my wet hand into hers. We were best friends.

"He's thinking," said Jeb.

Booth went to the rope then. He put a hand on the first knot, his other hand on the second knot, and began to pull himself up. All the way to the top of the gulch like that, slipping just a couple of times, but catching himself so the only real damage was the blisters on his hands and the mud covering him from neck to toe. As well as the fact that his Green Machine was now lost forever at the bottom of the mud pit, quickly filling with water.

Nobody spoke. We just looked at him—the rain was washing fresh blood from his knees and shin—us waiting to see, was it worth it? Was he sorry?

"Holy shit," Booth said. He didn't blink for a whole minute, even with the rain pounding at him.

Corrine and I looked at each other. She giggled so I did, too. Jeb said, "Oh, man!"

The four of us walked back up the alley to where the others stood watching us: three of us dragging our Big Wheels, one of us back from war, triumphant. All the other kids looked up to Booth already. He never said much, but whatever he did, you could trust. He had a big dog who walked around the neighborhood with him at his side, no leash at all, that was just her deal; Kizzy wouldn't leave his side for anything. Booth was almost ten and would be in fourth grade in the fall, so older than the rest of us and with no younger siblings to take care of or have to be nice to, he could take us or leave us whenever he wanted. When he asked them, "Are you ready to lose your Big Wheels?" we listened.

We looked at one another, at our Big Wheels.

"I just had the best ride ever," said Booth. "It's gonna be worth it."

"I don't want to lose my Big Wheel!" cried Cindy Fish, who was only four. She ran to her big sister, Wendy, who told her to go home if she was going to be a baby so she went back to her Big Wheel.

Booth went on, making his voice big to be heard through the rain. "Okay, here's what you're gonna do: You're gonna pedal out, fast as you can down the alley into the street then the crosscurrent will spin you so fast it won't even matter if you try to brake, you can't stop even if you try, you'll get thrown into that hole so fast you won't know what hit you. We'll need someone near the hole to signal up here when it's safe for the next kid to go, you know, once the last one's climbed out of the mud pit. There's a rope to climb out. Did I say that? Yeah, there's a rope. It's easy, just watch out for your hands. Ouch!" He held up his palms.

The kids made a hushed *ooh*, though there was little to see through that rain.

I nudged Booth, "Tell them that's where they'll lose their Big Wheels. I don't think they get it."

"Yeah, so that's where your Big Wheel will stay, I guess, forever."

"In the mud pit," I said real loud.

The little ones said, "Oh" and "Huh?" and "No."

"Kayla's right. But you don't have to do this," Booth said, "It's just the coolest ride and will probably never be possible ever again after today."

"I don't want to do it," said Clark Wills.

"Hey, man. No biggie," said Booth. He had this way of talking like a grown man.

"Me either."

"Me neither."

"I wanna do it," said Darcie Lynn.

"Cool," said Booth. "You'll love it."

"Me, too," said Arthur Beckwith.

"Yeah," said Booth.

"Me, too."

"Me, too."

"Me, too."

"Me, too."

And then it was everyone. Even Clark Wills and all the other naysayers.

Without Booth's Green Machine, the task of demonstration fell to me and my Big Wheel. And just like Booth said, I pedaled madly, sloshing down our alley, worrying maybe the rain had let up, that there wouldn't be enough to get me across the road. But just then, I hit the current in the street and spun out into it. My stomach flipped sideways and I thought I might throw up, but in a good way. Up over the curb I went, in a wave that picked me up and washed me down fast with a slam into the mud pit. My innards felt stirred around and my bones felt like they'd been jumbled up then rammed back in all the wrong places. The water was now about up to my waist. I got to my feet and tried throwing my Big Wheel out of the pit a couple of times, then gave up. The pit was too deep, the trike too heavy with water and mud filling the hollow wheels and seat, and the last time it landed on Booth's Green Machine, the handlebars locked with his steering sticks. I found the rope, now blending well into the wall of mud, and started climbing. Once out, I waved my arms at the top of the alley so they sent someone else down.

On and on it went like this, until the pit was so full of water and Big Wheels that we saw Corrine fly into the pit but didn't see her blue ponchoed head bob back up. We yelled for her but with the rain, who even knew if she heard us.

I would like to tell you I jumped in, swam through all the Big Wheels to find the person, the girl, the human being, my very best friend, and that she'd only been momentarily stunned beneath the surface of all that molded plastic. That I scooped up her head and brought it to the surface and patted her back enough to clear her airway and she breathed then climbed the mud-slimed rope to the surface and we sat huddled there a while reclaiming our strength but more alive than ever.

I would like to tell you that.

What I have to tell you is that we yelled for Corrine and

yelled for her and I felt sick to my stomach and hoarse, knowing I needed to jump in. Seeing how deep the water was now, I thought of snakes and even alligators because the water was pitch black. I crept slowly down the rope, inching, inching precious time away. When I reached the water, I felt for her with arms stretched out across the surface of the water as if playing Marco Polo at the Y. Finally, I had to put a hand below the surface, and she was there, right in front of me. Fingers, an elbow. Her head. Her mouth wide open. I screamed because I knew.

She was dead.

By now, there were more kids at the top of the pit. Dozens of shiny eyeballs peering down at me. I pulled Corrine up onto a stack of Big Wheels in the water, to lift her to the surface, but then it shifted and she went back under. I had to touch her again. Her shoulder. I dragged her back up again and again I floated her on top of another stack of Big Wheels. I held her in place by the billowed blue poncho. "Someone go get Booth!" I screamed up into the rain. The eyeballs only blinked.

What could he do, anyway? She was bigger, heavier, more unwieldy than a Big Wheel.

I climbed out.

Some put their arms around me. Some stood back.

Someone said, "We shouldn't have done this. I knew it was a bad idea."

"It's Booth's fault."

"I want my Big Wheel back."

"Me, too."

"Me, too."

I walked up the alley now, feeling each pelting raindrop and the hot wind. Back up to the starting line, where Booth had been waiting with all the kids before sending them on their way down the alley. All that rain? There was no way he could have seen what happened. So he hadn't. He just hadn't. "Booth," I said when I looked up and he smiled at me. "I need you."

His knees and shin were badly scraped and bloody and the blood had dripped into his right sock and shoe. Though the rain had cleaned his body of the mud by now, his clothing and shoes were still streaked with it, too. He told the three kids remaining to wait there, then said, "Come on" to me. We ducked next door to his house where there was a deck overhanging the garage to shelter us. He rubbed at his forearm. "Dang," he said, "now with a break from it, I can feel just how much that rain stings."

My teeth began to chatter.

"Hold on." He went inside his house. I looked down the alley at the pit. All those kids had left by now. I looked across the alley to the Butchers' house. Their living room light was on and the kitchen light. I wondered what Corrine would have had for supper that night. Her favorite was tacos and strawberry shortcake.

Booth was back. "Here," he said, pushing a Kilgore College sweatshirt at me.

I took off my poncho and pulled the sweatshirt over my head. "Why did you give me this?"

"You're cold, right?"

I shook my head. It was probably in the mid-eighties.

"Your teeth?"

"Oh," I said, holding my clattering jaw still. "Didn't anyone run up here and tell you—Corrine?"

He just looked at me.

"In the mud pit," I said.

"Can't she climb out?"

"I think she's dead."

"She's not dead."

"She is."

"She's not," he said, and I don't know why or how, but I believed him for a minute, and so I shut my eyes and realized my heart had been hurt and who knew if it could go on beating much longer like that, but now I was sure it would be okay again. Until he said, "What happened?"

And I saw it all unfold before me one more time: Corrine on her Big Wheel, Corrine spinning out in the street, Corrine flying through the air, Corrine falling into the mud pit, Corrine never coming up for air. Corrine, Corrine, Corrine.

I told him every bit of it, from the snakes and alligators to feeling my way to finding her open-mouthed in the muddy water and climbing back out without her. Booth looked at me, then he leaned his head to mine so our wet foreheads touched and we stood like this, forehead to forehead, eyes closed, all the while I saw stars inside my eyelids, me saying one word to him: *Corrine.*

When our eyes opened and our heads came apart, we were two people again. Booth said, "It will be okay." Then he went inside, where Kizzy tried to lick his bloody shin and knees, but he pushed her away and quickly ran right upstairs to tell his parents, tracking so much wet mud up the carpeted stairs.

I didn't want to go home. I went back to the mud pit and called out to Corrine. Then I just sat with her in the rain and let it bruise my back and head. Made a pact with the snakes that they could come for me, I deserved it. The gators, too.

By evening, someone had told someone else who told someone else who told Corrine's parents and another someone told mine and they all came to the mud pit with the police and a rescue crew to remove Corrine from the gulch.

Her parents wept. My parents cried. I cried. Booth and Kizzy came and watched and other parents came and some cried and others shook their heads or their children.

All these years later, mud still stains Booth's stairs and he and I are together, which my parents hate because he dropped out of high school and hasn't even gotten his GED and I'm on my way to nowhere if I marry him, they say. And probably they're right because I'm twelve days late and he waits tables at Gordo's, coming home stinking of taco chips and sloshed margaritas.

Mrs. Butcher moved away about eight years ago. Mr. Butcher still lives across the alley. Booth and I still live next door to each other. We're saving our money, especially now, though I haven't told him about the baby. I haven't told anyone.

I work at Brookshire's grocery and the library, and I'm going to start studying online next fall to get a BA and then my master's in library science. I'll probably only take one or two classes a semester, so it's going to take twelve years, but I'll do it.

This afternoon, I'm reshelving books when I come upon Mr. Butcher in 155.937 Grief/Death. He looks up and his face looks just as stricken as it did at Corrine's funeral.

"Oh, I'm sorry," I say, for interrupting him in a private moment.

He nods, his eyes retreating. He's unshaven, in wrinkled clothing, smelling stale and unclean.

"I really am so sorry."

"Of course," he says. He thumbs through the book in his hands.

"Mr. Butcher," I say, "she and I were friends, you know that." I touch his arm and he stops riffling the pages. "I'm pregnant," I say and now I whisper, barely making any sound at all, "and I'm going to call the baby Corrine."

His eyes rise to mine for a moment then sink back down. He leaves the book, turns, and goes.

At my evening shift at Brookshire's, Booth stops in. I think to tell him about Mr. Butcher but I don't want to say I'm pregnant over the conveyor belt checkout, so I wait. I ask my manager if I can go pee again and he thinks it's because Booth's here but, seriously, I need to pee. Again. I tell Booth to go on home and I go in the back and pee and make sure Mickey sees that Booth left. I do emergency pee runs two more times before my shift is over, buy a pee test on employee discount, then drive home where my mother is waiting at the dinner table for me with a big box, despite it being past eleven.

"Kayla, come sit here with me," she says. She's been to the salon and has her weekly hairdo freshly poofed, a motorcycle helmet of strawberry blonde hair all standing equidistant around her head.

"Now?"

"What do you know about this box?" It's dusty and stained, real old. She turns it around so the front faces me. It reads: "BABY CLOTHES."

My stomach tightens and I have to pee again.

"Mr. Butcher brought this by for you tonight."

I can't help it; I start to cry.

"What's going on, Kayla. Are you pregnant? You tell that awful man before you tell your mama?"

"'*Awful*'?"

"Don't turn this on me," she says. "He's been a drunk ever since his daughter's death and Judith left him. It's a wonder he hasn't killed someone, out driving like that."

I wipe my eyes. "Don't you feel any compassion for him?"

She pokes a long maroon fingernail up into the hair helmet to scratch her scalp. "Of course I do. Or I did. There's only so long you can go on having a pity party for yourself, then you've got to get up and make something of your life."

"I killed his daughter," I say.

She removes her fingernail and lays both hands fanned out on the table, her many rings clacking against the lacquered wood. "Don't be melodramatic, Kayla. Are you pregnant?"

I swallow. "I'm not even sure."

"But you're late."

I nod.

"What are you going to do? How will you support it on your paychecks? And no insurance." She holds up her left hand, running the tips of the acrylic nails against her thumb, back and forth, up and down the row of them over and over as she talks. "He said something idiotic about you naming the baby Corrine. You can't even know what sex the baby is right now, but even if it is a girl, you want to go and saddle her with a dead girl's name? That poor, poor child. You can't do that." Mom leaves the box and goes to bed.

I open one flap of the box and take out the first thing I see. It's a little yellow dress with squirrels sewn down at the hem. So small it almost fits in two cupped hands. I fold it gently and tuck it into my purse. I go next door.

Booth always leaves the downstairs door unlocked for me. His room is down here. I wait for my eyes to adjust to the darkness in here. Kizzy is white so she glows from the foot of the bed. She lifts her snout but doesn't get up; she's old. Booth's asleep. I slip in behind him underneath the covers, slide an arm between his arm and his stomach. I smell his hair, his ear, his stinky armpit, and drink him all in; I sleep like this until morning.

"Hey there," says Booth, wiping drool off my face.

"Oh, I got to pee!" I scramble so fast from the bed that Kizzy jumps up and follows me to the bathroom. "I'm sorry, girl," I say and shut the door in her face.

"You all right?" says Booth, once I'm back.

I nod, knowing I'm about to say what I'm about to say and not knowing how to say it.

"You sure are smiley," he says. He kisses me on the nose.

"So," I say. "So . . ."

"Yes?"

I mush my lips around from one side, then to the other side. I'm giddy with the hope of him loving me and this baby as much as I love it, her. "So."

"Yes?"

"So . . . I'm late."

"Late?" He looks at the digital clock by the bed. Then looks back at me. "Oh, *late*." He looks like someone who's just done the math with the right formula. Someone who doesn't enjoy math but has to take the class.

I nod. "Late."

"That's scary or, well, no—" he's looking at me and trying to see what I want from him, "—I mean, what do you want to do?"

"I love you, Booth. Don't you love me?"

"You know I do."

I exhale hard. "Can you just say it?"

"I love you, Kayla. You know it."

"Right but saying it and saying 'you know I do' are two different things. They make a big difference. Anyway, if we're in love, we have the baby. How could you even think we wouldn't? How could you even think that?"

"Sorry."

Kizzy stands up in her spot on the bed, walks a circle, then lies down again in the exact same spot. She grinds her teeth.

"We should take a pee test."

"Okay."

I get the box from my purse, careful not to let him see the yellow dress, and we go to the bathroom. I pee on the stick, we wait, two lines appear. It's official. I tell Booth about Mr. Butcher in Grief/Death. I tell him I think the baby is a girl but I stop there.

We don't tell Booth's dad for a week. Not until we see my mom and dad on their way over to talk and have to stop them, swearing his dad isn't home and he's had a really hard time at work lately, so many people being audited.

"For tax returns he prepared?" asks my dad.

I nod.

"That's not good," says my mom. "I hope everything's all right, Booth."

Dad tries to be tough on us for Mom's sake. He rolls his shoulders back and stands up taller than usual, saying, "A baby is about the last thing y'all need to be giving him, sounds like."

"Dad!" I say.

"Well, you'll let us know when things lighten up a bit for your daddy, Booth, okay?" she says. "That way we can talk arrangements. We will not have three generations under one roof and I bet he feels the same."

"You're kicking me out?" I say, running my hand over my girl.

"We can help get you started somewhere but then it's sink or swim," says Mom, clicking her long nails.

Dad touches her shoulder, like maybe he's saying *go easy* or maybe he's saying *I'm with you.*

I have a lump in my throat.

"That would be very kind of you, Mr. and Mrs. Davis," says Booth. He places his hand on my shoulder. "Kayla and I would really appreciate whatever help you can give us."

We go next door to his room and I try to swallow but all I can do is try to keep from crying. And it doesn't work. He puts his arm around me now. He looks at me and tells me it will be all right and what comes out through all my tears is, "We're going to name her Corrine."

"Wait, what?" he says, pulling down his arm to his side. "That's not funny."

"I told Mr. Butcher I would name—"

"You don't get to decide that." He moves from the bed to sit on the floor and Kizzy noses into his lap. He pets her face until she lies down all stiff-legged beside him.

"I thought," I say, "I thought we were the same about her. I thought we both wanted her back. And this was a way to pay a debt to . . . I don't know, the universe—"

"We're not paying a debt with our kid! Are you crazy?"

Kizzy rolls up on her elbows.

"I just mean that we could honor Corrine this way."

"That's not at all what you said." Booth hugs his knees. "You know what you said is totally fucked up, right? I mean *totally* fucked up."

We don't say anything for a while. Kizzy falls asleep, her paws flicking in a dream.

"We were kids," says Booth. "But of all of us, I was the oldest. I should have known better. It was my idea." He's never said this before and he won't look at me, just down at Kizzy.

"There's no way you could have foreseen it," I say. "And we were just kids. I'm the one who should have jumped in. I should have swum beneath the surface of the water feeling for her, I should have tried CPR."

"You didn't know CPR."

"I should have tried to get her out."

"Right, you were going to fireman carry her up the rope. Where were all the parents?" he says. "It was practically a hurricane. Why did they let us all play out back and down into the street with no supervision? We could have been run over."

"All those fucking Big Wheels," I say.

"I know, okay?" Still hugging his knees, Booth starts rocking.

"She'd have been fine if she hadn't hit her head on those fucking Big Wheels."

"Just shut up," he says.

I give it a minute then go to him on the floor. "I'm sorry," I say. "It wasn't your fault. It wasn't." I kiss him and whisper, "We'll call her Corrine and bring her back."

Booth takes on double shifts at Gordo's to sock away money for the baby and for a place of our own. I keep on at the library and Brookshire's, adding hours at the latter when girls call in sick or Mickey gets corporate to approve extra checkout lanes. Booth and I see each other only in our sleep and groggy morning goodbyes. We don't talk about Corrine. We don't talk.

Two weeks pass like this. Booth's dad leaves us a card on the bed one night. I'm home before Booth and there's no way I can stay awake until he gets here so I slide the card out of its envelope. On it is a picture of a pregnant belly with two hands on it, a woman's and a man's. It says, "Congratulations!" Inside, Booth's dad has written, "This may not have been planned, but what a blessing this baby will be. I'm here for you always. Love, Granddaddy Ford." I set the card on the nightstand and curl up with Kizzy in the bed, my hands on my girl.

In the morning, I dress for my shift at the library. I come

back in the bedroom to kiss Booth goodbye. I whisper in his ear, "Did you see the card?"

He groans and turns over. Kizzy lifts her head to me.

"Booth," I say. I squeeze his shoulder. "Honey, did you see your dad's card?"

His eyes flap open. "Card? Yeah."

"Wasn't it sweet?"

"Uh." He rolls over again and Kizzy lowers her head back down and sighs.

"Maybe we don't have to leave here quite so fast. Maybe we can save a bit longer, until we can afford something nicer. For the baby, you know."

Booth doesn't answer.

I go to work.

This is our life for several more weeks. Now I'm eight weeks pregnant and call to schedule my first prenatal appointment. I work. Booth works. His dad wants to take us out to dinner to celebrate but we don't have an evening off together unless we both trade shifts and Booth doesn't want to do that.

But this Sunday morning we can sleep in and then walk Kizzy together. We start down the alley, Kizzy right in step with us, with Booth. He takes my hand. My other hand is on my girl. It's a pretty spring day, with crocus bulbs wide open and hyacinths just having sprung. The air is crisp for Mineola, high sixties. So many of the kids we used to play with have moved on to college or moved away years ago and been replaced with new littler kids out now, playing on swing sets in their yards with moms in the kitchen windows, watching. It's hard to believe we ever did what we did. Or had the freedom to do it.

I squeeze Booth's hand. "Let's not walk all the way down, okay?"

"We can turn back," he says. "Come on, Kiz."

She turns with us. But she coughs. Then she stumbles. And then she's on the ground.

"Kizzy!" Booth says and he's on the ground with her, lifting her head but it's lifeless and falls back to the pavement. He pushes on her chest hard and air comes out through her lips but none goes back in. He opens her mouth and looks inside. He runs his finger around the back of her throat. He pushes her chest again, over and over, and the air moves through her but not really into her. He sets his mouth to hers and blows his own air inside her but she does not take it. Her eyes are open but they're not looking.

I kneel beside Kizzy and Booth, watching him try to resurrect his dog and fail again and again. Finally, I touch his arm. "I think she's gone," I say softly.

"She can't be," he says. "I've had her since . . . I've known myself."

"I'm so sorry, Love."

He scoops her up, this big beautiful white dog, and carries her across his arms back to his house. Every few steps, her body makes grunting sounds and he lays her down gently and checks her out all over again but it must only be the way he's carrying her creating movement and compression like breathing, so he scoops her back up again and continues. When we finally reach his house, he lays her down beneath a tall bur oak in the backyard, sets his ear against her heart, and tries chest compressions again. But there is no sound from her. No hope. He gets a shovel. I go for his dad, who comes with another shovel. They work without a word, just digging and wiping the sweat from their temples and brows. When the hole is four feet down and three feet long by two feet wide, Booth takes off her collar, and they lower her down gently, curled as if sleeping. Then they start filling the hole.

Booth calls in sick to Gordo's, so I call Brookshire's, too. He showers then collapses into bed, holding Kizzy's collar. He rolls toward the wall and I sit beside him, my hand on his back. I can feel him crying.

"At least she didn't suffer," I say, feeling stupid for saying anything.

He nods.

I lie down next to him and fall asleep with him but when I wake up needing to pee, I do it and then take my purse and drive to the mall in Tyler.

I go to Pea in the Pod and look at all the maternity clothes I'm about to need. I know I shouldn't, but I take one of their Velcro bellies and a couple of dresses in a fitting room and try them on to see how I'll look in six months. I fasten the belly's strap around my back and slip the first dress over my head. It's big flowers everywhere and I look like a sofa but I love it. I can't wait 'til my girl is this big, 'til she's here in this world, in my arms. My Corrine. I run my hands over the dummy belly, which feels strange because it isn't real but it's sitting on top of my girl, so it presses on her when I press on it. I try on the other dress, an aqua fit and flare with small daisies all over it. I decide to get this one. I just need this in my closet. So I get it and go home.

Booth is still in bed when I get back, but he's awake. I go in the bathroom and change into the dress. I ball up my shirt and jeans to make a belly and come out to show him.

"Like it?" I say.

He looks up from his pillow. "That's weird."

I try to smooth the lumps out of the belly. "It's how I'll look at six or seven months."

"Okay. It's pretty."

"Thanks." I drop the clothes from the belly. "It was on sale," I lie. I unzip the dress and pull it over my head.

"When do you start to show?" He sits up in bed, rubbing at his red eyes.

"Should be any day now." I pull up my jeans and zip and button them.

"I guess you're lucky you can still wear all your clothes, huh?"

I grab my shirt and pull it on, too. "Yeah, I guess."

"Thanks for the show," he says.

I give a little bow and lean in and hug him. "How are you doing?"

"It'll sound ridiculous, but it's worse than when my mom left." He wipes at his eyes again to keep from crying.

"Oh, Love. I'm so sorry. She was the best dog ever."

He nods. "She was." His voice cracks. "There can never be another dog like her. She knew exactly what I was thinking every second of the day—whatever I needed, she gave it. She was perfect. Not just the no leash thing, though that was cool and you know I never trained her for that, she just did it on her own."

"I know."

"And if I was sad, she got goofy. If I was angry, she calmed me down. If I had a hard day, she relaxed me. If you and I fought, she'd lie on top of me. Whatever it was, she was there to fix me. How am I ever going to find another dog like that?"

"You will, if you want to. And if you don't, I can be goofy when you're sad and help relax you when you've had a hard day and all that."

"You can't be my safe haven from you," he says and pokes my nose.

"Um, okay."

"You know what I mean."

"Yeah, I do. I'm so sorry she's gone."

He wipes his eyes again and his nose. Booth takes a deep breath and lets it out. "Okay, so when's your prenatal tomorrow?"

"At 8:15. You're still coming, right?"

"Of course."

Without feeding and walking Kizzy, Booth's morning routine has him sitting at the table over his empty bowl of granola, drumming his fingers long before I'm ready to go. But once we're in the car, he's less agitated. The doctor's waiting room is packed with pregnant women of all ages and all trimesters. I imagine myself as each one of them, with each of their baby bumps and popped-out belly buttons. We wait forty minutes before the nurse calls us back. She has me first step on a scale, then go in a bathroom and give a pee sample. Then Booth and I go with her into an exam room, where she takes my blood pressure and goes over my medical history and form of birth control. She asks the date of my last period and the age of my first. Then she asks me to undress and put on a gown with the opening to the front, she leaves, and I do so. Now we wait again.

"Do you think she'll think it's weird I'm sitting where I can see right up into you?" says Booth.

"She'd probably think it was weirder if you didn't."

The doctor comes in and she's short and cute as can be, with long brown hair, a round face, and rainbow-striped socks with her blue scrubs. "I'm Dr. Zelly," she says, pulling out the stirrups for the table and guiding each of my feet into them. She runs through an initial exam: listening to my breathing, palpating my breasts, and doing a pelvic and cervical exam. "Are you experiencing any cramping?"

"No," I say.

She swabs my cervix, snaps the end of the swab into the specimen vial, and screws the jar shut.

"Any spotting or bleeding?"

"No."

The nurse comes back into the room with a big machine. Booth pulls his feet up out of the way.

"We're going to ultrasound." Dr. Zelly pulls the machine around to the other side of the table. She types into the machine, then takes the wand out of its holster, squirts lube on it, and slides it into me. "Some pressure," she says. "Sorry, it's cold."

"It's okay," I say.

She's looking at the screen, her eyes sort of squinting.

I look at Booth but he's looking at Dr. Zelly and the screen. She's moving the wand all around inside me to find things, then she stops the ultrasound picture and moves a cursor ball around on the machine to measure points across each thing. White zigs and zags arc the screen.

She does this all over me inside until she says, "I'm sorry, guys, we should be hearing a heartbeat if you were pregnant. There's no gestational sac."

"What?" I say, but I may not have made any sound.

"It's what we call a chemical pregnancy. When the embryo doesn't implant or grow."

"So, she's not pregnant?" says Booth, leaning forward like to see the words on the screen.

"No, there's no pregnancy," says Dr. Zelly, looking at him, then at me. "I'm sorry."

"Did I do something? To miscarry?" I ask.

"No," she says, "you didn't do anything to cause this. An embryo that never implants is just cells sloughing off, not a fetus."

"Why haven't I gotten my period?"

"There are all sorts of reasons that we can definitely pursue—being on birth control can sometimes cause . . ."

I look at the ceiling, which has posters of fat, happy babies in daisy fields with puppies, breastfeeding and sleeping in a mother's arms.

". . . even stops entirely for a while. There's also stress as a culprit. Thyroid issues. Low body—"

I look to the right wall, where there is a photograph of Dr. Zelly in surgical scrubs, holding triplets.

". . . start with some blood panels and go from there. It's probably the pill and you're perfectly healthy and your period will return on its own, but we should check all the boxes we can to be sure."

She turns to Booth and back to me but who am I, where am I, I don't know.

"You two should use condoms so you can get off the pill and give your body a break from the hormones, see if that solves the problem. Sound like a plan?"

THE MUD PIT

My teeth start to quietly chatter.

She fills out the form that I'm to take to the checkout window, then leaves. The nurse cleans the ultrasound machine and wheels it out. I wipe away the lube and dress.

Booth is looking at me, but I don't look at him. I grab my purse and he stands. But he grabs my arm. "Wait," he says. He holds me now. Forehead to forehead but I can't hear him think her name. When he's done, I walk out the door feeling untethered—not quite floating, not quite weighted, just somewhere unknown in between.

At the checkout, I decline the tests and a follow-up appointment.

I drive Booth to Gordo's, unsure how we got here once we arrive.

"Let me call in again," he says.

"It's fine," I say. "You just did for Kizzy. We need the money, and besides, I have to work, too."

"You're sure."

I give him a smile.

"I know that's not real." Still, he gets out of the car. "Just call if you change your mind. That's all you have to do and I'm there." He leans back into the car and kisses me. "I love you," he says. "I love you."

I drive. But I don't go to my shift at the library. I go to his house. I park out front and then I just walk along the street side of our houses, down to the cross street, down to the mud pit.

Where I sit at the edge and wait. I put my hand on my stomach and, at first, I think I feel her. But I know how stupid that is.

I look over the edge of the hole. "Corrine," I say, "I've never had a best friend since you. Except for Booth, but that's different. And he had Kizzy." I think of us braiding each other's hair after school. Of us swapping sandwiches at lunch, peanut butter and jelly for salami and swiss. Of us catching fireflies in pickle jars with nail holes hammered into the lids. "I've never even truly had a friend besides you and Booth." I thought maybe, just maybe, my girl could . . . I don't know.

I thought of the rain stinging our backs, our arms, our heads. All of us in our colored plastic ponchos. The whooshing cross-current sending her up and over the curb and down into the pit so full of all our Big Wheels. The water so deep and black with mud. Corrine underwater, not coming up. Corrine lost. Corrine dead. Corrine gone forever and me too scared to help her in time.

I'm sobbing now but it's self-indulgent, and so, I wipe my eyes, my nose. I swallow all this hurt up inside me again. My own Corrine, too. My own Corrine. I get my breathing back under control and I go walking up the alleyway but not to my house or Booth's. I go to Mr. Butcher's house. I knock on his back door. He opens it and stands there with both hands, palms up, a man who doesn't know what to do with himself.

"She's gone," I say, crying again, my face wet and nose dripping. "She's gone and I'll never get her back."

Mr. Butcher's stubbly face crumples. He turns and leaves

me here in his living room. I stand in the doorway a moment, ashamed to have been so thoughtless. I wipe at my eyes again and again, but the tears keep coming. I step inside and shut the door. There are dirty dishes on nearly every surface, old food grown fuzzy with mold. I take the plates to the kitchen. I scrape the food into the trash and leave the plates to soak. Years of dust coat all the surfaces in the living room, including Corrine's first-, second-, and third-grade pictures on the stone wall. Her in a green dress and pigtails. Her with french braids and a silly grin. Her in a light blue top with colorful embroidered flowers, her hair cut short and pushed back in a white plastic headband.

I check his refrigerator. There isn't much, but I thaw some ground beef in the microwave, brown it, and put together a lasagna. Once I get it into the oven, I wash and dry the dishes. Then I go looking for Corrine's dad.

"Mr. Butcher?" I call out, my voice quivering.

He doesn't answer.

I go upstairs, find him in Corrine's room, which is perfectly clean and just as it was when I used to come over to play and spend the night. He's sitting on the bed, his hands, palms up, on his thighs.

I stand in the doorway.

"At some point the world wants it to stop hurting." He shakes his head. "It never will. Not 'til the day we die."

I take a deep breath so I can make it out of here in one piece.

"Kayla," he says.

I'm backing out of the room. I'm running down the hall.

"Kayla!" He's coming after me. "Kayla, stop please."

I stop on the stairs, my back to him.

"I meant that to be of comfort," he says.

"I made you a lasagna."

"Nobody's ever cooked for me—not since Judith left. Thank you."

I turn around and see his blue eyes are the color of Corrine's: Texas sky blue. I'd never noticed that before, and I suddenly realize I've been picturing my Corrine with eyes that same shade and it's another little death again.

"What was she like that day?" he says.

I shut my eyes. Shake my head. "I hardly remember anymore," I say. "We were so young." I start down the stairs again.

He follows me down, but lingers at the foot of the stairs.

"Was she nervous to do what y'all were doing?" His voice goes low and tight. "Was she afraid?"

"She was beautiful," I say. "She was fearless."

"Oh, god." He takes in a sharp breath and holds a fist to his mouth.

I go to the kitchen. "What would you like to drink?" I call. There's no alcohol anywhere in this house, no matter what my mother says. He doesn't answer so I fill a glass of water. "Go sit," I call and take him a square of lasagna and a glass of water. Mr. Butcher stands wet-faced, fussing at the family table with the many piles of mail and paper that cover it. He lifts a few pages of one pile, then sets them back down only to lift a few pages of the next pile and so on and so on, never moving any of the piles out of the way.

"Can we temporarily relocate one or two of these so you can eat here, Mr. Butcher? How about I just set this one on the floor here and then we can set it back up here when you're all done?"

He nods so I move two piles and he sits.

"Aren't you having any?" he says. "Please Kayla, share this with me."

"No, I made this for you to have leftovers."

"It's no good eating alone. Please." He picks up a pile at the next chair and places it on the carpet out of the way, too. "Besides, you're eating for two now."

I look away. "Right, okay."

I get a small piece and we're quiet eating. When we're done, I take our plates and his glass to the kitchen and wash them.

"Have you looked through the box yet?" he calls out to me. "I don't remember Corinne's baby clothes much. It will be nice seeing them again on your Corrine."

I slip out the back door.

Out into the alleyway, where I stand stock still, waiting to know which way to go—to my home, to Booth's, to the library's 155.937, to the mud pit. Or do I just go out to the front of our street to my car and leave all this behind me, heading out to a world where I might find a friend or a love without mud climbing inside. I slip my hand down into my purse, feeling around for my car keys but what I come back with is the little yellow dress instead. Just barely big enough for two hands, the sight and feel of it makes clear to my heart.

I take out my phone and I call him, say for just the second time in our lives, "Booth, I need you."

The Suicides

When the suicides start in my kindergarten class, they're just a game. Last Sunday, Krista's grandmother pulled a radio into her bathwater to prevent the Parkinson's going any further, so the kids now sit straight-legged on the play mats, pretending to run a washcloth over their bodies, then tug a length of yarn onto which they've pasted large construction paper squares and rectangles that read CLOCK or HAIRDRYER or TOASTER. Now they really ham it up. They go into all sorts of convulsions to simulate being electrocuted, smashing through their imaginary bathtubs right into one another, until they are finally out of energy and breath in a pileup on the mats. I let them sleep it off in place and when they wake, one by one peeling themselves from the pile, I rebraid, recomb, or repony their hair and tell each one in a whisper, "Suicide is forever. It isn't a game," and they go sit in their seats, looking glum.

Krista is at the bottom of the pile and, so, is the last to wake and the last I rebraid and tell, "Suicide is forever."

She turns around so fast her hair burns the palm of my

hand. "It's not," she says on the way to her seat and the class perks up. "There's Jesus and heaven. My mom and dad say so."

"Okay," I say, because I know the surest way for a teacher to get fired is to fuck with Jesus. "I just mean your grandma can't come back to earth."

"She can if she wants," says Tegan.

"Can if she wants," says Ally B., swinging her legs under her desk.

"What does that even mean?" I say. "In what way could she possibly come back?"

"Jesus came back," says Krista.

"Well," I say, "that's debatable. But also remember that not everybody in the room believes the same thing your families do. It's important to respect *everyone's* beliefs."

"Who doesn't believe in Jesus?" says Lipman, holding up his hand and looking around the room. "Raise your hand."

"No, don't raise your hand," I say. "We're not giving friends a religious litmus test."

"What's that?" they say.

"A Jesus test," I say.

"I'd pass," Brian calls out.

"Me, too," says Quinn.

"Me, too," says Finn.

"I'd pass," says Min, but I know her family is Buddhist.

"You know I would," says Goldy.

"Stop it!" I say. "Children, stop it! You don't need to prove your Christianity. In fact, doing so is hurtful to others. You're setting yourselves up as a powerful ruling class against a silent and powerless minority. And that's scary."

"We don't know what you're saying," says Arthur.

"I think you do," I say, shutting my eyes for a moment.

"She's saying we're being like our parents," says Ally T.

I pop my eyes open again. "Exactly," I say, but Ally T. has her pigtail in her mouth and is looking out the window.

I turn off the light. Min passes out the cups of juice I pour, and Finn distributes the graham crackers. They sip and nibble in silence. I don't tell them not to talk but they must feel the need for quiet, for thinking things through, because no one says a word.

Afterward, though, we go outside and I seek out the second-grade teacher, who is not quite a friend but someone I talk to at school on days like these. His kids have the kickballs and jump ropes out, and they share with some of my kids. Kyle and I stand around the edge of the cafeteria wall, which blocks a bit of the view, because he vapes and can't let the children or roaming administrators see.

"Did you watch the game last night?" he asks me.

"No." I don't even know what sport he means. This is March, so basketball? Baseball, soccer, volleyball? I haven't a clue. I read at home with my dog on the futon next to me. Or I watch baking shows. That and affix colored stars to handwriting and phonics worksheets. That's truly all I do.

"It was a good one," says Kyle. He sucks on the vape pen. "They took it in overtime. It was tight."

"Sounds exciting."

Electronic smog comes out his nose. "You know it."

I decide not to tell him anything. "I'd better go check on my class."

"See ya."

I round the corner and make my way through Kyle's taller students, and then I see it. Krista, Finn, Quinn, Min, Brian, Tegan, Goldy, Ally B.—half of them with jump ropes wrapped around their necks, the other half standing on the jungle gym trying to hoist the ropes up to hang them. I run to stop them, to keep them from being seen and keep the hangings from progressing any further.

We go back to the classroom. I say, "I told you 'suicide is forever.' What's wrong with you? What's going on? This isn't funny."

"We aren't joking," says Brian.

"Then what are you doing?" I ask, rubbing my own neck where they have red marks from the ropes' plastic beads.

"We don't know," says Min.

"We don't see a point anymore," says Tegan.

"A point?" I ask.

"Why we're here in the first place," says Quinn, shrugging.

"To learn and prepare for lives as informed citizens of the world," I say.

"No," says Krista, "she means why we're here on Earth. Why we're even alive."

"I see." I don't see. I don't see at all. Several of the kids rest their heads on their desks, but they all look to me for an answer I don't have. "Some say death is what gives meaning to life."

"Yes, dying!" says Robbie.

"No," I say, "not the act of dying or how you die—just the fact that it will happen means you have to fit all the good parts of living into a limited number of days."

They stare at me.

"You can only eat ice cream every day of your life that you're actually alive, do you get it? Once you're dead, you can't eat it anymore." I move around to the front of my desk and sit on it. "Let's try this: your best friend moves away but she's coming back to visit for four days."

"Why is she a girl?" Robbie asks.

"Because you're not a jerk," I say.

The kids laugh; Robbie pouts.

"Okay, now listen, everyone. She's coming to visit for only four days. Won't those four days be the best days? And won't the days afterward feel long and tiresome? Won't you feel bored and lonely on those days after she leaves?"

"Where are you going with all this?" asks Finn.

"My head hurts," says Min.

"My head hurts, too, Min," I say. "What I'm trying to say is—I don't know." I sit down behind my desk with my face in my hands. "I've become tangled around and all I really want to say, I guess, is please don't die."

———————————

The next day, Krista brings in the program from her grandma's funeral. In the morning playtime between drop-off and Vocabulary, the children bury one another under heaps of their coats and shoes, the dress-up clothes, books, and magnet blocks. All across the classroom floor are these strange burial grounds, with maybe a blue-socked foot poking through or the tip of a brown braid, until there is only one student left standing.

It's Min. She packs the last of a game of checkers, board and all, around Tegan's face then comes and stands in front of me. "Kill me?" she asks.

"Oh, Min," I say and I sweep her long, black bangs out of her eyes.

"It's okay." She lies down in between a mound of princess dresses and another of milk carton bird feeders. She closes her eyes.

I look around for whatever's left but the room is bare. They've used everything that wasn't nailed down. All in their quest for death, their quest for meaning. And who am I to say they're wrong? Maybe death is transformative or transcendental and not just nothingness.

I drape my grade book over Min's middle and I lie down next to her. I shut my eyes and imagine the dirt piling up over top of me. I lie here listening to the children breathing, their little inhales and exhales, so warm and moist like puppies.

And then there are faces over me. Krista and Goldy, Arthur and Robbie. "You were asleep," they're saying. "You fell asleep." "Do you know you snore?" "You do."

I sit up and try to stand, but they're kneeling on my skirt. I move them back and start to rise but stop. "What if I hadn't woken up?" I ask.

"Then we would have woken you," says Arthur.

"And if you couldn't? If I weren't simply asleep?"

"We would go get the nurse," says Goldy, her clammy hand on my arm.

"That's a good idea," I say. "But what if I had died in my sleep?"

They come flying at me from every side now, landing on me, knocking me back onto the mat, sitting on my knees and feet and hands. "Then we'll love you forever and ever and ever!"

"We'll always say a prayer for you before we go to sleep, every night," says Brian.

"We'll name daughters after you," says Quinn.

"If we live that long," says Min.

"Is that what this is all about?" I ask. "If I die, I become famous to you?"

"If we die, don't we become famous to you?" they ask.

The next day, all of the children look like French poets, dressed in black head to toe. I don't ask. Ally B.'s mom drops her off with jellybeans and cupcakes for her daughter's birthday. After the kids eat the cupcakes, they decide the jellybeans are pills. They overdose and die in their seats. Tongues lolling out of their mouths. Bodies sprawled across their desks. I think of my dog Betsy curled up beside me, of TV dinners and streaming *Nailed It!*, and the sensation the red star stickers make when they cling to my fingertip instead of the worksheets. I collect the empty juice cups and crumby cupcake plates. And I begin to prepare the whiteboard for the morning's Vocabulary lesson, but, instead of chapter 31.2, the words I write on the board are: *dead, grave, tomb, mausoleum, funeral, cemetery, pyre, kamikaze, wake, shiva,* and *suicide.*

There is a tug at my elbow.

It's Min and she tries to smile now, looking up at my words.

Suddenly I'm full of shame. I turn my back to the board, try to block as many of them as I can. She's a good reader and her eyes study them, seem to imprint them.

"Will we need to know these?" she asks.

I turn back around with the eraser and smudge them all out. "No," I say, "these are—no, they're not for you. They're not for class."

"It's okay," she says. "We always come back."

"What?" I say. The board is clean again.

"Buddhists," she whispers.

I turn back around to her and Min smiles again. She returns to her seat. The rest of the class is coming back to life, as well. They stretch and yawn, wipe the drool from their chins and laugh at one another's death sprawls.

No Matter Her Leaving

Charlie joined the circus when she was only twelve. She took my dog Mouse, and the neighbor boy, though he came back at the end of summer with a tan and a foul mouth. Charlie and the dog sent a postcard from Flagstaff then from Salt Lake City then Laramie then White Sulphur Springs then Eugene. The picture on the front was always the girl being shot from the cannon. And that was Charlie.

I have another dog, a sweet blue pit called Malone. He's doleful without Charlie and the little mutt anymore. He won't get in my truck with me to ride for groceries or go to my store or even just to go for a drive. He'll sleep all day, on the porch or in my chair or my bed. It's hard getting him to eat now and his ribs are starting to show.

I have another daughter, Tina, but she's older and doesn't often come home. She's nineteen and out of school. I can't keep up with where she's working each week. Sometimes a bar, sometimes an earring store, sometimes a florist. Their mother, Colette, left us when Charlie was four.

This morning, Malone lifts his head when I get out of bed. He turns to follow me out of the room.

"Come on, lazy bones," I say, looking back at him. "Today, you're coming with me."

He lays his head back down.

In the kitchen, I pour some kibble in his bowl. I shake it all around, making as much of a rattle as possible. Still, I know it's just kibble and he won't get excited for that. I open the fridge. Grab an American cheese slice. Crinkle the wrapper a bunch. "Hey Malone, want some cheese?" I picture his head up, ears perked. "Want some cheese, good boy? I've got cheese for you. Who wants cheese?"

I hear his big body lope off the bed and shuffle into the kitchen. He comes and sits in front of me.

"That's right, good boy." I tear a piece of the slice and give it to him and he takes it but gingerly, manneredly. This poor sad dog. "I miss them, too," I say. I give another piece of cheese. He takes it and swallows. I give him the last or try to but he just walks away, back to the bedroom.

I make toast and coffee, get cleaned up and dressed. "Okay, Malone. Time to go to work. Come on now."

He sighs and curls in a tighter circle on the bed.

"Malone, it's time to go."

Nothing.

I get the leash from the side door and clip it to his collar. His eyelids squinch tighter.

I give a little tug to get him started but it only unfurls him from his sleeping circle. I tug again and again, this last time a bit harder. "Come, Malone," I say.

He's upright on the bed, at least.

One more good pull and he's walking out of the house with me. Or at least he's off the bed and I can keep tugging him along. I hate this but I get him all the way to the truck and now lift him up and in. I own a SavRLot convenience and gas at the corner of Wayne and Pickins. Malone used to always come with me. All summer, though, I've let him stay home. Until today.

Once in the truck, getting Malone out is the hassle. He's fast asleep so I leave the windows rolled down to the cool fall air and open the store and the pumps, change out all the outside trash cans while he's still in the truck. He starts dreaming and it's like he's a new kind of bird making his *boof boof* calls in the parking lot.

Both of us wrap up about the same time so I lock up the truck and lead him into the store. We're not there two minutes before he's sacked out on the cool tiles behind the counter with me. I make fresh coffees and start the hot foods. A bunch of junior high kids come in before school with one fake college ID—someone's older brother's—trying to buy a Juul.

"You have to be eighteen in Indiana," I say. "Sorry, that's the law."

"Daaaamn," says one of the kids in back.

"Roasted," says a curly-haired one, laughing.

"But I am," says the kid, pointing to the ID.

I look at the picture and at the boy. "That's not you, kid." I shake my head. "I could lose my license."

"Sell it to *me*," says another boy. "It looks more like me."

"That's not how this works," I say. "I'm not selling tobacco of any kind to any of you."

"Daaaamn," says the one in back again. "Hey, when's Charlie coming back?"

The curly one pushes to the front. "Is it true she's the girl gets shot out of a cannon?"

"Don't believe everything you read in the funnies, boys," I tell them.

"See," says the one in back.

"Fucking Simon," says the one with the ID.

"No?" The curly boy needs to hear it again from me.

"Well, actually." I pull out one of her first postcards. The one from Salt Lake City.

The boy leans down, studying it. "I mean, that could be anyone," he says. "Is it her?"

"Yeah," I tell him, "it's her."

The boys crowd around the postcard but the curly one doesn't give way. "That's cash money," he says. And the rest are impressed, too. Eventually, they tear him away from the card and go on to school and Malone has slept through the entire exchange.

At least a dozen people pull their cars in for gas on their

way to work and pay at the pumps without any trouble. I restock the napkin dispensers for the afternoon rush, refill the cups and lids, too. Then step over Malone to go back to my stool.

Stretched across the hard tile, Malone's ribcage protrudes mightily. Almost like he's one of those abused dogfighting-ring dogs who's never been fed or touched, to make them mean. I step over him again and go grab a can of Vienna sausages, peel back the ring top, and pour out the liquid in the prep sink.

"Malone," I say, patting him on his side. "Here, boy." I hold up a sausage and he lifts his head in slow motion. He sniffs it and opens his big square jaw, then closes on it. I hold up another and he takes it, too. "You like those, don't you? Want more?" I give him another and another until they're all gone. "Good boy," I tell him. "Good boy."

I stand up to throw away the can just as Sheriff Hurley comes through my door. My stomach goes queasy. He takes off his hat and runs his other hand through his hair. The sheriff and I played football together in school. I wouldn't say we were friends but we weren't not friends and he's been kind to me over the years.

"Lewis," says the sheriff, holding out his hand.

"Sheriff," I say, shaking it.

"We need to talk."

"Okay."

"Colette's gotten herself in trouble again."

"I see," I say. I look down at Malone sleeping. He didn't have this kind of reaction when Colette left and I wonder why not, since she doted on him. "How much will it cost?"

"She stole . . ." he takes his notepad from his shirt pocket, "$1,289."

"Who from?"

"Employer," says Sheriff Hurley. "Same story. She was working as a domestic and got hold of his checks. Wrote a whole slew of them before he caught on."

"Why was she back here? She said last time she'd leave for good."

The sheriff just shakes his head.

"Twelve hundred and eighty-nine?" I write down the figure on a square of scratch paper.

"You got it." He flips shut his notepad and pockets it.

"And if it's repaid, you go away, right?"

"He'll drop the charges, he's said, yes."

"And what about her? Is she ever going to leave?"

"She swears all she wants is to get a fresh start someplace new."

"All right," I say, "come by the house tonight at 9:30."

"Will do." The sheriff holds out his hand so we shake again. He replaces his hat and goes.

"Goddamn it, Malone!" I shout. "Goddamn!" He lifts his head now and I see I've still got the sausage can in my left hand and did all this time. Fucking idiot, I am.

I throw out the can and pass the rest of the day slowly then quickly then slowly again. I feed Malone another can of sausages. When it's time to close up, he stands of his own will and I am grateful. He lifts himself into the truck and curls up next to me on the bench. At home he climbs down, walks inside, and goes straight to the bed.

Thankfully, Tina isn't home. I go to the closet in the bedroom, to the safe there. Open it and move the gun and the deeds to the house and the store out of the way; below is my entire life's savings, or what's left of it after all Colette's legal doings, to which I've contributed some or all because she's the girls' mother and somewhere in me is a love so deep for her it's dangerous.

The girls don't know. That's the deal I strike with Colette each time, and she swears she will not contact them. As if there's any chance she would.

I count out what she needs this time and seal it in an envelope for the sheriff. While I wait, I scramble eggs with breakfast sausages broken up in it. A whole mess of them. Two plates. I take both to the bed and let Malone eat his there. I sit and eat mine on the bed, too. When the sheriff rolls up, we're nearly done so I let Malone polish off my plate, too, and I go let the sheriff in the side door.

"Smells good in here," he says, taking off his hat and adjusting his hair.

"Just trying to get my dog to eat."

"Hell, that's for the dog—*I'd* eat that!"

I show him the envelope. "Here it is," I say. "And you're sure this finishes it. Drops the charges. Nothing more, right?"

"Yep, she'll be free to go."

"And she will *go*, right?"

"To the best of my knowledge," he says.

"All right." I hand it to him.

He slips the envelope inside his jacket. "Thank you, I'm sure." He turns to go then looks back and says, "Now that it's fall, at some point we're going to have to talk about Charlie and school."

"She's doing correspondence classes," I say from who knows where. "Likes them a lot. Has all As and a B⁺ in French right now. She's doing great."

"Oh, well that's super." He replaces his hat. "I can check that box then, can't I? You have a good night."

I watch the sheriff's car leave the drive, its heavy tires spitting gravel the entire way. My pulse is in my throat, spitting and popping along with the gravel. It's against the law to lie to a sheriff, right? I'm pretty sure. *Correspondence classes.* All he has to do is place a phone call. Just ask the question.

I pour a bourbon. Okay, it's done. Nothing to do now but start believing Charlie really is doing correspondence classes and forget I ever had that $1,289. I drink the liquor and feel it burn going down. I move to start cleaning up the stove and skillet and Malone is here.

"Hey, boy." I pet his head, scruff him behind his ears. "You up for a walk?"

But he turns around and goes back to bed. I hear the plates clatter to the floor.

I'm on the side porch with another bourbon when Tina walks home. She's on her phone so I hear her long before I can see her. And I hear and see her way before she sees me.

"That is so cool!" she's saying. "No way! Even higher? Oh my god! Yes!" She waits, now, "Are you kidding? What did she do next? No!" And Tina laughs then goes quiet. "Oh, that's so sweet. That is like the sweetest thing in the whole wide world, oh my god. I love it." She steps onto our porch and suddenly sees me. "Ach—Dad!"

"Who are you talking to?" I ask.

"No one." She rolls her eyes.

"Is it Charlie?" I reach for the phone. Charlie has never called me. Not once since leaving home. And she doesn't have a phone so I can't call her. You would think there was some big fight that precipitated her departure, some new rule or curfew to balk at, but there wasn't. We always got along famously. I could get her to come back, of course, and legally I know I'm supposed to, but I can't bear to think of her unhappy with me. Of one more heart I love leaving me forever. My Charlie girl. She'll come home when she's ready. She has to. She will. I ask again, "Is it her?"

Tina holds the phone at arm's length away from me. She shakes her head. "I've told you, Charlie doesn't call me."

I go in the house, go to bed. I know when I'm beat.

The next day, Malone won't leave the bed at all. I fix the leash on him and give a gentle tug but he splays his legs in the doorjamb and lets out a mewling sound like a cow in a slaughterhouse. I don't have the stomach to keep going. I carry him outside to do his business but he refuses and finally I have to carry him back inside or I'll be late to open the store. He shuffles back to the bed. And when I get home, there's shit and pee in the corner of the room. The floor is only linoleum and what did I expect so I don't yell at him. I clean it up and fry us burgers for supper.

Tina comes in late, bumping into furniture and dropping things. I get out of bed and knock on her door.

The bumping and dropping stops.

"Yeah?"

I open her door a little. "Malone had an accident today. When you get up tomorrow, please take him out."

"Don't you take him to SavRLot?"

"I didn't all summer. Haven't you noticed he's been here with you?"

"Sure," she shrugs, blinking slowly. "I know."

"Please take him out when you get up, okay?"

"Don't you take him out?"

"Is this too much to ask, Tina?"

"Fine."

"Thank you," I say. "Good night."

"Night." She pushes the door shut.

I push it in again. "Charlie really has never called you? And you never call her?"

"Uh-huh." Tina nods.

"I miss her so much."

"Why didn't you go after her?"

"Does she want me to?"

"I'm not saying that—how would I know?"

"I guess I figure she needs to get this out of her system."

"She's twelve."

I nod.

"Is she allowed to have a system?"

I can't lose her, too. "She'll come back when she's done."

"What makes you so sure?"

———————————

But fall becomes winter and Charlie turns thirteen on a postcard sent from Crystal Bay, Nevada. No phone calls or return addresses. The bedroom linoleum is starting to curl in the corner and the subfloor will need ripping up and replacing from all the pee and shit. The smell singes my nostrils and throat. I just can't get Malone outside, and if I carry him, I can't get him to potty there. I bought puppy pee pads and put them in that corner, I even taped one up on the wall for when he lifts his leg up, and they help but the damage is extensive.

Some nights I dream I follow her out west. Dream I'm sitting inside the red-and-white striped tent when they roll out the cannon and out she strolls in a sequined leotard, cape, ballerina slippers, and top hat. Miserable elephants trudge circles inside the far left ring; in the center ring, a pitiful lion stands motionless while tiny poodles form a pyramid atop his back. Lining the rings are the crudest of sideshow acts, all writhing: snake men, bearded ladies, contortionists in knots upside-down, Siamese twins, monkey boys, and flaming sword swallowers. But in the far right ring stands Charlie, waiting next to her cannon, arms alternately extending, showing off her cape. A tall man in a red-and-white striped tuxedo and top hat appears with the cannon. He lowers the nose of it and Charlie takes pointy-toed steps to it, just like she did coming out of the wings at every ballet recital. She removes her top hat, revealing what looks like a sequined bathing cap, and unties her cape, showing off bright red sequined stars on her front and back. She hoists herself up and slides her legs down into the cannon. She swivels around and lowers her entire body, arms extended out in front of her, like in the postcard, a graceful swimmer poised to dive. The crowd hushes but she pops back up just enough for her right hand to wave goodbye. The crowd laughs, but it's a nervous laughter, and now we fall even more silent than we'd been before.

The tall man positions the cannon upward again, getting the angle just right for the trapeze net, I suppose. He shows us his jar of matches. He takes one out. He lights it and holds the flame to the fuse. The sideshows grind harder. There is a spotlight on the cannon and a drumroll.

Some nights I wake here. And it's as though I can't breathe and won't breathe ever again. Some nights she hasn't gotten into the cannon yet and I can live with that, watching her show off the sequined cape and silly top hat.

But there are a few nights when she explodes from the cannon and the spotlight crosses the darkness of the tent and I'm not even sure what I'm seeing except for the bright red star and two satin-slippered feet and then they land. But not in the trapeze net, no. They land on the back of one of the elephants who is transformed, made somehow glorious by Charlie's arrival. Charlie stands, both arms skyward, and she and the elephant parade through the ring, never happier.

I know the reality of it is something different but the two could share some similarities and that's what I hope for. And that my Charlie will tire of it and come home. That she will need me, or at least want me. That she will want me, or at least need me.

On the night I come home and can't even rouse Malone with porterhouse, I make the decision. It's December 29th and Tina and I didn't even exchange presents in person because she spent Christmas with a new guy she's seeing and only came home for fresh underwear. Charlie didn't come home for Christmas, so she's not going to come home. No Charlie, no Mouse. Malone doesn't move at all anymore. He shits in the bed, he pees in the bed, he sleeps in the bed. I put down towels across the sheets in the morning. I put down new towels in the evening. His eyes are sunken. His ribs, feet, and tail are all that's left of him. I open the fridge, grab a stick of butter, Velveeta, and raw chuck. I get a mixing bowl, turn out all of it inside the bowl.

"Malone!" I call. "Malone! I got yummy grub." I leave the bowl on the countertop in the kitchen and grab the leash. "Hey, boy." I stroke his face. Sit with him a minute. Stroke his side, what used to be muscly back. "You're all tendons and bones now, boy. I'm sorry," I say. "I'm so sorry. I did all the wrong things, didn't I?" And I break down. Malone picks up his head and lays it back down. He licks my hand once. His tongue is dry, almost feels like a cat's sandpaper. I pet him. "You're a good boy with a broken heart. You're such a good boy."

I go to the safe. I get the gun.

I carry him to the yard, set him down, and go get the bowl. When I set it down in front of him, he's not interested. I pinch a bit of the ground chuck and hold it to his nose. He opens his lips. I tear a bit of cheese and do the same. I split a bit of butter away from the cold stick and offer him that. He licks it then gently takes it with his teeth. I offer him the whole bowl now that he is upright. He sticks his nose in the bowl. Have I found something he can love?

But Malone sighs and rests his head on his paws. I sit with him. I offer him another pinch of chuck but he won't have it. "Everybody leaves," I tell him. "Everybody but our own selves and that's no consolation."

NO MATTER HER LEAVING

I sit myself behind his shrinking body, stroking his jagged backbone from neck to tail, and when he starts heavy breathing and his feet start flicking around in a dream, I shoot him through the head.

The next day, Sheriff Hurley comes to the store, saying, "We need to talk." He takes off his hat and his other hand goes to fix his hair. It's one of those mannerisms that always comes next so it drives you crazy on a day like today when nothing matters except the things that truly do.

"What is it?" I say too sharp.

"You all right?"

"Sorry. What is it?"

"Colette's in some real trouble this time."

"I'm not in the mood for this," I say. I leave the register to dump the coffees and make fresh for the afternoon rush. "Surprise, surprise she never left."

"Now listen, Lewis. She's had a scrape and she may not be able to brush this off too easy."

"What is it?" I slam the fresh pots under the drips and wipe down the counter.

"Come on back over here now, you're making me nervous."

I go to my stool behind the counter. "What? What did she do? I'm sick of this and sick of her and I've half a mind to let her problems be *her* problems from here on out."

"Lewis, just hear me out and you can decide if you want to be involved or not. It's totally up to you, of course." Sheriff Hurley presses his palms flat on the counter. "She's looking at some time, though."

I shut my eyes. "Of course she is."

"She's been living with this real bad guy. He's mean. We've been out to his place for years and we take him in but no one ever presses charges. Sometimes we have enough on him, so we can hold him and even give him a little time but not much. Anyway, she's been with him since about, well, since before she ran those checks—she was with him then."

"Oh great."

"This guy, his name's Dell Perty, he broke her cheekbone—"

"Shit."

"—and tailbone and what's that outer bone in your forearm that abusers are always breaking by twisting gals' arms so hard? Well . . . that one."

"The ulna?"

He nods. "He broke that one, too."

"So why is she the one looking at time?"

Sheriff Hurley looks over his shoulder, though the bell on the door hasn't rung. "Because she killed him."

"Jesus fucking Christ, Stew!"

The sheriff puts his hand on the counter between them. "Now it's only manslaughter," he says, "and we're waiting to see if the prosecutor wants to go voluntary or involuntary so there

could be good news there, possibly great news. I think maybe
you'd like to see her, maybe help her out with an attorney—
court-appointed versus one you get can make all the difference
between conviction and freedom and I think maybe you'd a lot
rather have her on the outside. All these years you and I been
meeting like this, helping her out, you haven't seen her—"

"I don't want to see her."

"And maybe that's how you'll feel tomorrow, too, but maybe
you'll sleep on it and wake feeling differently. Maybe you'll wake
feeling like she's the mother of your girls and that's worth something to you—"

"Fuck you, Stew. Just fuck this! You don't think I've done
enough? You don't think I've been enough of a stand-up guy?
I've raised our girls by myself. Been their dad and their mom.
Fed and clothed them. Kept them clean and safe and happy and
home."

"Well . . ."

"You think she could have done any better? Then where
was she? I was here. I didn't run off, I didn't go steal from
everyone I ever worked for, I didn't count on my ex to do it all
for me and then clean up my shit. And I didn't kill somebody.
Jesus!"

"You understand manslaughter, Lewis?" he says.

"I understand it just fine," I say. I think of Malone last night,
wondering what gradation of the law the sheriff would make of
the bullet in *his* brain. "I understand it."

He unzips his jacket, takes a card from his uniform pocket, and lays it on the counter between us. "You want to bail her out, you go here tomorrow after she's charged."

I leave the card where it is.

"She's the girls' mother," he says. "She didn't ask for this."

He takes his phone from his pocket, taps and swipes through some screens, then lays it down on the counter. "I've got to use your restroom, Lewis. You mind?"

"In the back."

"Know it well."

A woman comes in for Tide. I ring her up and bag the detergent.

"Who's that?" she says, grimacing at the sheriff's phone.

I grab it and the card and put them behind the register. "Sorry," I say.

She turns to go.

"I'm sorry," I say again.

I pick up his phone just as the screen dims but I know by that woman's reaction what it is. I touch the screen and Colette's face comes back on: fresh reds, purples, pinks, old greens, and yellows. Her face looks older but who knows what is injury and what is age. Her hair is still strawberry blonde, her left cheek swollen, her hazel eyes frightened.

"You want me to text that to you?" The sheriff is back. "Officially I can't because it's evidence, but I can screenshot it and give you a copy."

I hand back the phone. "If I want to help with a lawyer—"

"First things first, call the number on that card and get her bailed out."

———————————————

In two days, I've paid $25,000 and Colette's sitting on a hemorrhoid pillow on my sofa. She's sipping a Diet Coke and answering my questions with yes or no, being sure to say *please* and *thank you* when I offer her another Diet Coke or a little bowl of peanuts, which I remember she used to like with her pop.

When I sit down in my chair next to her place on the sofa, it's like nine years ago, like fifteen years ago, and we're in our old spots sipping drinks and looking at each other. Except her left arm's in a neon yellow cast and I can't stop staring at the colors of the left half of her face. They've gone browner and spread since Sheriff Hurley's photograph.

"What hurts the most?" I ask.

She picks up the bowl of peanuts and sets it back down. "Maybe those aren't a good idea," she says and motions to her busted cheek.

"Oh, sorry. Yeah." I try to think of soft finger foods but can't come up with any.

She picks up a hank of her hair and runs the ends of it between her lips. "Where's Malone?" she says.

I get up, take the peanuts to the kitchen, and dump them out. I call to her, "Want some yogurt?" I pour a bourbon and drink it up. I pour another. I walk back to the living room with my drink. "What was that? Do you want some yogurt?"

"No," she says. "No, thank you." She's looking around the room. Like maybe she just didn't see him. "He's still alive, though, right? We got him when Charlie was . . ."

"A year before you left us."

"Okay. Yes, so he's only ten years old," she says. "That's not too old."

"Uh-huh."

"So where is he? Malone?" She's turning this way and that. "Malone?"

I sit back down. I drink my bourbon. "Were you afraid when you killed a man?"

She turns back to face me. Her eyes fix on mine. "I never knew you for a cruel one, Lewis."

"A lot can happen in nine years," I say. "You just never know." I take another sip.

She looks at me and I can see something I never saw all those years we were together. Like in her photograph. She's afraid. But of me. I reach out for her hand, saying, "I'm sorry," and she flinches.

I go get my coat and stand out on the porch until she's gone to bed in Charlie's room and I can go hide in my own bedroom, too.

She stays in bed in the morning, which gives me great relief. I leave a note for her born of my shame. Just the word "Sorry" and then I get out of there as fast as I can. At the store, the lawyer calls me and sets up a meeting between the two of them so I have to call her at the house.

"He's coming at two o'clock, okay?"

"Okay."

"I'm home about ten after nine tonight."

"I remember," she says and we hang up.

When I pull in the drive, there are lights on in the house for the first time since Charlie left, and at first, I think it's her who's back. My feet quicken up the porch steps. Then I see Colette's mottled face in the kitchen window. She gives half a smile, waiting for me to reciprocate before she'll give the other half. I open the door and slide out of my coat. She doesn't speak. She's at the sink. The oven is warm, there's a pot of something simmering on the stove.

"You cooked," I say.

"Thought you might like that."

"What is it?"

"Pork chops, potatoes, and braised cabbage."

"You need any help?"

"I'm all right," she says, washing her good hand, her back between us.

I go to wash up and I notice pieces of furniture have been moved but put back, just not exactly in the right spot. Bushel baskets of magazines or blankets here and there are swapped for each other and don't make sense—like the one full of blankets is in the bathroom now.

I come back to the kitchen. "What did your lawyer say?"

"He's confident. Because the prosecutor went with involuntary, he thinks their case is weak to begin with."

"All right." I open a bottle of Chianti.

Colette sits on her donut pillow and chews only on one side. The food is good. The wine goes fast. Colette could always cook.

"You want another helping?" She scoops into the mashed potatoes and takes my plate.

"No, girl. I'm done." I scoot my chair back. "That was real good, though."

She drops the spoon and stacks our plates.

"You sit," I tell her. "I'll get all this." I scrape her plate of bone and fat onto mine for Malone. Then remember and dump it all into the trash. I pull out the bottle of bourbon and hold it up. "Want some?"

"A little," says Colette, passing a rope of hair between her lips.

I pour our glasses and finish clearing the table but just leave everything heaped on the kitchen counter. I come back to the table and sit there again, sort of collapse there so we laugh at the sound I make. Colette covers her mouth, sort of turns away laughing and then turns back to me and when her hand drops back down to the table, I don't know why or even how, I take it. There's only so strong one man can be. I love her. I always have, no matter her leaving. There's a wound but the heart still beats.

I lead her down the hall to the bedroom and there she stands before the highboy dresser and I stand before her. I undress her. Her blouse and jeans, her bra and panties. Careful around the cast, her cheek, her tailbone. Even in the dark, even nine years later, touching her skin is like touching a live wire. She climbs under the covers and lies down on her right side. I strip quickly and get in beside her. I'm all hands all over her like a college student or maybe now that's high school. Her one good hand is on me, stroking me. I kiss her—softly, so softly so as not to hurt her cheek.

I stop. "How does this need to work for you, baby?" I say. "I don't want to do anything bad for your tailbone."

"I think you've got to come at me from the front like this." She squares up my hips to hers now lifts one of her legs over my hip and leads me inside of her.

I can't pretend I last longer than I do. I've only dated two other women in the nine years since Colette left and neither for very long or very recent. And neither one ever compared to Colette.

"I'm sorry," I say, rolling away from her and cleaning myself in my shirt from the floor.

"That's okay. It was real nice." Colette wipes up with Kleenex and then sits facing me with an extra pillow placed under her rear end.

"It's just, it's been a while."

"I understand," she says. "What happened over there?"

"Oh," I say. She's looking at the corner where I ripped up the linoleum.

I get out of bed. Go to the safe in the closet right in front of the bed. Behind me, the coils in the mattress shift. I type in the code and take out a shortbread tin. I turn around with it and Colette is there just over my shoulder, propped on her elbows, at the end of the bed. I sit next to her and place the box in front of her. She opens it slowly, finds Malone's worn blue collar and tags, a picture of him as a puppy with a big wormy belly, the blue yarn that identified him among his littermates at the shelter, and the cartridge shell. That is the last thing Colette picks up.

She doesn't say a word, just holds it up to me so I start at the beginning of summer when Charlie and Mouse left and Malone first grew despondent. By the time I'm done, what I want her to do is bang her fists against me and tell me I'm a monster, but she kisses me, says, "It was no kind of life. He was begging you practically."

"Yeah," I say. "I guess that's so."

I come home with flowers from the store, a nice wintry mixed bouquet for Colette tonight. Some mums and greenery, I don't know. I pull in the drive and the lights are on in the kitchen. I wonder what she'll have cooking. Her chicken and dumplings were always a favorite. I'll have to put in a request.

I come up the porch, push in the door, and she's not in the kitchen. And nothing's cooking. I slide out of my coat and go looking for her in the bedrooms but she's not in ours and she's not in Charlie's. She's not in the living room and not in the bathroom. And she's not doing laundry. I sit down at the kitchen table to think if maybe she told me of some meeting with the lawyer or some other late-night errand.

And then it hits me.

I go to our bedroom. I key in the combination to the safe and open it up. I pull out the shortbread tin and the deeds to the house and the store. And that's all there is. The gun is gone. My money is gone. And Colette, of course, is long gone.

———————————

From bed, I hear Tina move through the house like a wrecking ball. She thinks I'm at the store but I haven't opened it in several days. She blasts her music, bangs cupboards, rolls through the hallway, thumps into the refrigerator, and clatters her dishes into the sink. It doesn't matter. None of it matters.

I fall back asleep but then she barrels through my door. "Oh my god!" she says. "You scared me. Why are you here?"

"I don't—why are you in my room?"

"I'm running a load of wash. Why aren't you at your store?"

I make a small sound. "I just can't."

"Are you sick?" Tina asks.

"Yes, I'm sick."

She looks at me now, studying me. "You look mangey but you don't look sick." She closes the door and that's the end of it.

I barely eat. I drink water and get up to pee once in the

morning and again at night. I poop once a week. I sleep and doze and simply exist with my eyes shut. I lose track of days.

Then one day there is a knock on my door and in walk Charlie and Mouse. I think I'm hallucinating because of how strange Mouse's fur feels to my fingertips and how long it takes my eyes to adjust to the light. Charlie is taller now. She has freckles draped across her cheeks and nose and her brown hair is nearly to her elbows. She's wearing smudgy gray eye shadow and has started to develop breasts. She shows me pictures on her phone that Simon took when she was first training in the cannon and then progressing to her first shows, being photographed all artsy by a girl named Stella. Tina elbows her and winks and Charlie blushes so maybe my daughter likes a girl. I think of that poor curly-haired boy.

Mouse flops down on the pillow next to me. She's tired from her journey but I think she knows about Malone. "At least there's no gun in the house," I whisper to her.

"What?" says Tina.

"We need to get you up and moving," Charlie says, pulling my hand up but I don't budge. "Malone!" she calls.

Tina cuts her eyes to her sister. "No," she says. "*Veet.*" She drags her finger across her throat.

"Where is he?" says Charlie slowly.

"He's fine," says Tina. "He's just not here. It's okay." She pushes Charlie. Gets her bustling again. "Go get the stuff."

"Okay, yeah, the stuff!" Charlie hops off the bed and runs to the kitchen. She must have just dropped her bags there. When she comes back, she's got a wrinkly sack of genuine circus popcorn. "Nothing but the best!"

I reach in and take a few pieces. Mouse gets a couple more that drop.

"Et voilà!" Charlie takes another wrinkled sack out of her coat pocket, this one is filled with peanuts in the shell.

I crack one and eat the nut. Tina and Charlie toss popcorn to each other. Mouse inches down the bed to position between them and snatches a few more pieces.

Tina's phone buzzes. "I'm out of here."

"Nice knowing you," says Charlie, who gets up and follows her out.

Mouse goes, too.

I reach to flip off the light, turn onto my side so I'm looking at Malone's corner where I tore off the linoleum and the paint's still streaked with urine.

"Daddy?" Charlie sets her small hand on my back. I quickly sit back up.

"What is it?"

"Am I like her at all?"

I pat the bed next to me and she sits. I hear skittery claws on the floor and she lifts Mouse back up to the bed, too.

"Who . . . Tina?" I say.

"Mom." She takes in a deep breath and holds it.

"You're not a single bit like her. Not one single bit."

She's quiet a minute considering, then lets her breath go and breathes in again.

"Not at all?" she says, leaning her head to one shoulder. "Not even a tiny bit?"

"You came home."

"Are you going to be okay now?" Charlie asks. "Since I came back? You'll eat and go to your store now and be normal, right?"

"Right as rain now that my Charlie girl is back home," I say. I've just got a little flu or something is all. I'll be all right tomorrow, I'm sure of it.

She smiles. "Okay," she says. "Good." Charlie takes a hank of her hair and runs it between her lips.

My stomach drops. "Do you think you'll . . . are you going to stay now?" I ask.

"Tina says I have to."

"Well," I say, "there's the law. You're a minor and all that. So technically speaking . . ."

"But I really love it, Daddy."

"What about school?"

"Oh, I'm in school. I do correspondence classes."

"You're kidding."

"No," she says. "Truly. I'm already in ninth grade."

"Maybe I could come out and see you?"

"Oh, yes! I would love that. You've never shut the store before. I didn't think you could leave it."

I rub Mouse's belly and she rolls on her back. "Well, we'll

see. I'd sure like to see you jump from a cannon."

"I'm *shot* from it, Daddy. I get shot! And it's the most exhil-arating feeling ever."

"All right, Miss Cannonball Charlie! Time for bed."

"Night, Daddy."

"Night, Sweet girl."

"Daddy?" she says, turning back to me.

"Yes?"

"Is he dead?"

"Yes, honey. He's dead."

"Oh, Daddy. I missed seeing him. Missed saying goodbye." The tears spill down her cheeks.

"I know, sweet girl."

Charlie and Mouse curl up with me in my bed. They're out so fast I'm still not even used to the dark again. I pick the pop-corn from my molars and fall asleep thinking of food, which I suppose is a good sign. Of meals to come, of sustaining a body, of not wasting away like Malone. And when I dream, I am back at Charlie's big top, but I'm not in the stands. I am the tall man in a red-and-white striped tux with tails and top hat with the cannon, leading Charlie into the ring, taking her cape and her own top hat. There are no grotesqueries lining the rings in this dream. There are the lion and poodles and there are the elephants but they are not miserable. And there is one more animal in the far ring. There is Malone, his coat sleek and body muscular. He trots in between the elephants, prancing in the opposite direction, his physique rippling, his tail wagging high. I light the fuse and the drumroll begins. An elephant sits and Malone scampers up its back to now ride high upon its shoulders. The elephants continue their parade around the ring and they are majestic. The lion regal. And he, too, parades with the poodle pyramid on his back. The cannon booms and out flies the shooting red star of Charlie to land perfectly atop the elephant carrying Malone. The crowd roars and the elephants trumpet and I walk to the center of their ring, letting Charlie and Malone and nine elephants holding trunks to tails turn around and around and around me until they are all I see and all I know, all I want to see and all I want to know, here where I didn't shoot him and here where I never ever lose her.

ACKNOWLEDGMENTS

These stories first appeared, sometimes in slightly different versions, in the following publications: *Confrontation, CRAFT Literary Journal, Green Mountains Review, Moon City Review, Peatsmoke Journal, Split Lip Magazine, Spoon Knife 5,* and *storySouth.*